THE GREENHOUSE MYSTERY

THE GREENHOUSE MYSTERY

NORVIN PALLAS

WILDSIDE PRESS

To Kimberly

CHAPTER 1.

LADY BEE

IT was mid-June, and the car sped along the graveled country road, as though it, too, were celebrating the end of another successful college year. Nelson Morgan was at the wheel, his ubiquitous camera deposited carefully on the rear seat. Beside him was Ted Wilford, summertime reporter for Forestdale's small but justly famous *Town Crier.*

"Isn't it great, Ted? Three whole months before we have to burn the midnight oil again. I was really worried about that final calculus exam, but everything came up roses." He glanced quickly at his friend, who was making some notes on questions he wanted to ask Mrs. Bowen, co-owner of the Lady Bee Floral Nursery, whom they were to interview. "I've had my head in the clouds for two days. You want to clue me in again on this roses deal?"

"The Forestdale Garden Club has decided to participate in the Loki Pageant of Roses this year, and Mr. Dobson wants me to work up some background material."

"I'm with you that far, Ted, but Loki is in the opposite direction, remember? All you said was, 'Get your camera and pick me up at the office,' and I came running."

"Mr. and Mrs. Bowen are the largest suppliers of flowers for local florists in this part of the state. I believe they usually take the lead in the Loki Pageant, and sometimes they come up with some surprises."

"What kind of surprises?"

"New roses, I suppose. I understand there are thousands of different kinds, and more coming along every year."

"That so? It's probably like almost everything else—it turns out to be more complicated than you expect, once you get into it. 'Lady Bee Floral Nursery.' " Nelson thought it over for a few minutes. "I suppose the Lady Bee is Mrs. Bowen—that would be a pun on her name, wouldn't it?"

"Yes, I imagine she's well known for doing the kind of work that bees are usually thought of as doing."

"I wonder why I never heard of these people before?"

"Because they're not much interested in selling directly to the public. But they do have a fine rose garden and a conservatory which attract a great many visitors."

Nelson let out a groan. "*Now* you tell me, and I'm stuck with a black-and-white film in my camera." The *Town Crier* never used colored pictures.

"Suppose I *did* tell you, what could you have done about it?"

"Taken along two cameras. I've still got my big old press camera, besides this little baby."

They had a seventy-five mile drive, during which there was ample time for Ted to review everything he knew about greenhouses, flowers, and roses in particular. He liked to be as well prepared for an assignment as he could, but there had been little time, nor was Nelson able to add much to his store of information.

"I've heard about the greenhouse effect. The sunshine comes through the glass, and the heat is trapped inside. That's about all I know. I suppose the idea of a greenhouse is to grow plants that otherwise couldn't be grown in this climate, or else to grow some of our regular plants out of season."

"Yes, and probably to protect some of the more delicate seedlings and plants that might be hurt by storms or hail. How many roses do you know?"

"After you mention American Beauty, you've lost me."

"And I don't know much more," said Ted, wishing he had paid a little more attention when some of his mother's friends had spoken with her about their gardens. But there was no help for it now, and when he and Nelson had both contributed all the little sniplets they could remember, the conversation switched to other things.

The Lady Bee Floral Nursery announced itself with an attractive road sign which directed them down a country lane. When a turn of the road brought the estate into view, their first impression was that of dazzling sunshine from the late sun reflected off the slanting roofs. But the cluster of long greenhouse buildings formed only a part of the operation. Many more acres were devoted to open fields in which at least a dozen widely-scattered workers could be seen. There was another building, too, much more ornate than the down-to-earth greenhouses, though it was also constructed principally of glass panes.

"That must be the conservatory," Ted observed. "That, and the rose garden around it, are open to the public, though I don't believe the greenhouses themselves are. I suppose they put all their showiest flowers in the conservatory, and the greenhouses are where the real work goes on."

Though they drove past the conservatory and the garden, they could see very little beyond the high hedge, and a sign told them they had missed the afternoon conservatory hours and were too early for the evening. After turning up the drive which led to the office, they parked in the small parking lot, then walked over to the office door. A young woman sat at the desk whose name plate announced her name as Clarice Lance. She looked up with a smile.

"May I help you?"

"I'm Ted Wilford," said Ted, stepping forward, "and this is my friend, Nelson Morgan."

"Oh, yes, Mr. Wilford," and Miss Lance also nodded toward Nelson. "Mr. Dobson called from the paper and told us to expect you. Mrs. Bowen is somewhere in the greenhouses. I'll buzz her."

"Don't bother her if she's busy. We have plenty of time."

But she pressed a buzzer which apparently resounded at a number of different places in the buildings, and presently Mrs. Bowen came on the phone.

"She'll be down in a few minutes," the secretary explained, replacing the receiver. "Make yourselves comfortable, and if there's anything I can do for you, don't hesitate to ask."

There were so many questions Ted would have liked to ask that he hardly knew where to begin, and it was Nelson who spoke up.

"Is this a family operation? It seems almost too big for that."

"Well, the place is owned by the Bowens, and their son was active here, too, before he went away to college. Everyone else you see around the place is an employee."

"Then Mr. Bowen isn't just a drone bee?"

The secretary was used to jokes about the name, and her polite smile was forced. "Oh, Mr. Bowen works very hard, but he is on the road a good deal. He claims that he doesn't have Mrs. Bowen's instincts with the flowers, and prefers to handle the business end. Of course there are always customers and suppliers to call on, and rivals to watch, and like all rose breeders, he keeps his eyes open for any attractive wild roses he happens to encounter on his travels."

"Wild roses?" Ted questioned. "Aren't they almost obsolete by now, with all this breeding going on?"

She laughed. "If a man was in the business of building brick homes, would he think bricks were obsolete? Wouldn't he keep alert for any new kinds of bricks, at the same time using the bricks he has to build many different kinds of homes? Well, wild roses are our original bricks, and the whole business, originally, was built upon some thirty wild species. Of course they have been crossed and re-crossed until there are now many thousands of different kinds."

They had not noticed Mrs. Bowen enter the office, but she had heard the latter part of this conversation. After she pulled off her gloves and shook hands with the visitors, she picked up the same theme.

"Yes, we must never scorn the wild roses, even though it often seems we have come a long way from them. But they have their own kind of beauty, and I'm not always too sure that we have ever truly surpassed them. Even now there are gardens devoted to old roses, though even these may be hybrids. It's hard to know just what roses were originally, for even those we consider wild do not breed true. If we were to breed them indiscriminately in their wild environment, they would eventually revert to their original state, but it would take a long time, and we might never be sure when we got there."

It was the end of the day for Miss Lance, and having cleared her desk, she asked if there was anything further.

"No, Clarice," Mrs. Bowen assured her, "run along. I'll lock up later."

A green roadster had pulled up in front of the office, and Miss Lance was hurrying out the door when Mrs. Bowen called after her, "My Canadian cuttings didn't come, I suppose?"

"No, they didn't."

Mrs. Bowen sighed. "I guess I just thought I saw the express truck."

Miss Lance got into the car, and she and her escort drove away. Ted, eager to complete his interview as quickly as possible, returned to his list of questions.

"Mrs. Bowen, a reporter isn't supposed to admit how little he knows, but the truth is I know very little about flowers, and I know I couldn't fool you for long. Still I hate to ask you a lot of stupid questions. Do you suppose you could just tell us a little about your roses?"

"I wouldn't mind at all, Ted. It's my favorite subject, so that usually I'm afraid of boring people. Without question the rose is the world's favorite flower. A florist has told me that about half the people who come into his shop ask for roses, and most of the others ask, 'What would you suggest?' and many of them end up buying roses, too. Without roses, or something equally popular to take their place, the florists might just as well quit.

"The remarkable thing about roses is that they do not breed at all true from seeds. If you plant a rose seed, something may come up which bears little resemblance to the flower from which it was taken. Should you develop a very fine rose, you would not propagate it by seeds, but rather by a cutting or similar method. On the other hand, the seeds are very useful for developing new varieties. You could plant thousands of them, and hope that perhaps one would come up that would be different from and better than anything grown before. Different they would be—you could at least have the satisfaction of knowing you had roses that were different from anything else on earth—but whether they were commercially valuable would be the problem."

"Having to make thousands of trials just to produce one good rose seems a tremendous waste of energy," Ted observed. "Isn't there any short cut?"

"I don't know of any," Mrs. Bowen answered. "You see, we are dealing with two different kinds of building materials—the male and the female—and we don't really know what either of them consists of. As long as it is so much work to produce a new rose, you can understand why our government protects our rights to it with a patent."

"Do you have such a rose coming up for the Loki Pageant of Roses?" Ted questioned.

"Yes, I have a rose which I call Governor Hope—for the governor of this state has given me permission to name the flower for him. I am quite pleased with it myself, but I will wait till I see how it makes out in the show before deciding on a patent. It is a lavender, and in my opinion it is superior to Sterling Silver, Orchid Masterpiece, Song of Paris, and Lavender Charm. Still, it is a fact of life that lavenders seldom win the top prizes, and so I will have to reserve my enthusiasm."

"I bet people think a rose ought to be red," Nelson pointed out, "and it should climb a trellis and have lots of thorns and a sweet odor and bloom in June."

"You may be right, Nelson. Final judgment does depend on what people expect. One of the top prize-winners, Peace, is a yellow-to-rose color blend, and that fulfills part of your theory. Peace is usually barred from the 'open' categories so that it won't walk off with all the prizes."

"May we see Governor Hope?" Ted requested.

"I'm sorry, Ted, but we fumigated that greenhouse today, so I am unable to show it to you."

"Mrs. Bowen." A man stuck his head in the door. "I've told Tony Thorton to fertilize the northwest quadrant tomorrow morning. Shall we use 6-10-4?"

"No, I think 5-10-5 might be a little better, Mr. Gompers. Did you notice the express truck going by today?"

"Why, yes, I did. They brought your Canadian shipment. They didn't want to maneuver up the drive with that big truck, so I sent it up with a boy. Didn't you find it?"

CHAPTER 2.

POISONED AIR

AN air of tension immediately settled over the small group. Ted and Nelson gathered that this package was of considerable importance to Mrs. Bowen.

"Which boy was it?" she asked, her voice restrained.

"That red-haired boy, Freddie."

"Freddie Barker. Is he still around?"

"I saw him a few minutes ago standing out by the road, waiting for his father to pick him up. He may still be there."

"I'll go get him," Nelson volunteered quickly.

The others stood in a silent group until Nelson returned with a boy of about fourteen.

"Freddie," Mrs. Bowen began, making an effort to sound casual, "Mr. Gompers tells me that an express package arrived this afternoon, and that you carried it into the office. Can you tell me just where you left it?"

Freddie looked at her with wide, anxious eyes, as though fearing he had done something wrong but not quite sure what it was.

"Yes, Mrs. Bowen, I brought it in and put it right on the desk. I suppose maybe I shouldn't have done that, but Miss Lance wasn't in, and I wanted her to be sure and see it. Did I get her desk dirty?"

"No, you did just right, Freddie. The package was gone by the time she returned, but I suppose someone has simply put it away somewhere."

"I really did put it on her desk," said Freddie earnestly.

"I'm sure you did, Freddie. Don't worry about it. Now you had better run along and meet your father."

After he had gone, Mr. Gompers suggested, "Maybe Miss Lance put it away."

"No, I asked her, and she didn't know anything about it. At what time did the express truck arrive?"

"It must have been about three-thirty."

"Yes, that would check. Clarice was out of the office for about twenty minutes beginning at three-thirty. She wanted to meet some friends at the conservatory, and I told her it would be all right. You're certain it was the Canadian shipment?"

"Oh, yes." Mr. Gompers withdrew a yellow express receipt from his pocket and handed it to her. She looked it over, nodded, and placed it on the desk.

"Was it a very valuable shipment?" Nelson inquired.

"I suppose it wouldn't have a very high *monetary* value," Mrs. Bowen replied, "but in terms of trouble in preparing the shipment and the time lost in replacing it, it is very valuable to me. This thing we were talking about a few minutes ago, the genetic building bricks we use to create new varieties—it has been thought by many experts that the best chance for introducing new material into our roses would come from wild, hardy, sub-arctic species. A friend of mine did this for me, and added some of his own hybrids—and he did this, not for money, but as a personal favor. It might take another year, and a strong imposition upon a friend, to make up a similar shipment.

"And then there is the problem of U.S. customs. When a shipment such as this comes through safely, you breathe a sigh of relief."

As she spoke, Ted had been looking around the office carefully. Obviously, there was no place where a large bundle such as they had described could be concealed. There appeared to be two entrances into the office, the front way they had used, and a rear door.

"Where does this door lead?" Ted questioned.

"Why, nowhere, right now. I'll show you."

She opened the door into a short hallway. Except for a small washroom off to one side, the corridor ended abruptly with a closed door bearing the sign:

Danger
Fumigants
Do Not Enter

"What if people don't believe in signs?" asked Nelson.

She smiled in reply, and indicated that he try the door. He did, and found it solidly locked.

"It is bolted from the inside. No one could possibly go through the door from this side, without breaking it down." She turned to her superintendent. "Who did the fumigation?"

"Tony Thorton handled it himself. He was through about three o'clock."

"Was he alone? You know I don't like anyone working alone on this. In case of accident there's no one to help."

"I usually direct him, but Jerry was off today so I was needed outside. I'll watch it next time."

"Is Mr. Thorton working out pretty well?"

"Oh, yes, he's still pretty green, but beginning to catch on."

"At least no one could have come through here after three," she said, turning away.

They returned to the office, and Mr. Gompers took his leave.

Once more Ted looked around the room. There were several windows, open but with screens that were hooked from the inside. One side looked out upon the parking lot, while the other side gave a view of the conservatory and rose garden. If the package had been stolen shortly after three-thirty, there would have been numerous visitors in the garden and the parking lot.

"What about these fumigants?" Nelson was asking. "Are they very dangerous?"

"Well, Nelson, I would much prefer to do without them if we could, but if you want to grow roses on a commercial scale, you need poisons. If a pest gets started in a nursery, it may soon wipe out your entire stock, and you are out of business."

"You do take precautions?" Ted suggested.

"We do everything that we can to make them safe."

"Then I suppose we can rule out the idea that anyone walked the length of the greenhouse, stole the package, and walked back through the greenhouse," Nelson reasoned. "How valuable would this package be to anyone else?"

"Not very. I shouldn't think anyone else would want to bother with it, or would know what to do with if it he did. If you should plant these roses, what you would get would be inferior roses, by our standards. But you would also have the hope that, by crossing them with others, you would get something superior and unique. A great deal of our business is based on hope."

Ted's thoughts were running rapidly along another channel. "Mrs. Bowen, apart from this missing package, has anything else unusual happened lately?"

She considered carefully. "It's strange you should ask that, Ted. Several days ago Miss Lance told me that she thought someone had broken into our office safe during the night. There was only a small amount of money in it, plus our office records, and nothing seemed to have been disturbed."

"You would think a thief would have taken the money, even if he was disappointed at the amount," Ted remarked.

"Not if he decided to call if off and come back another day," said Nelson with a laugh.

"Do very many people know the combination to the safe?" asked Ted.

"Miss Lance is the only one, except for my husband and myself—and my husband was out of town at the time."

"Suppose it wasn't the money but the records the person was after. Would there be anything of value to him?"

"I can't think how. There are our regular bookkeeping records, and our customer records, and our operations records—but I don't see how any outsider could benefit from them. If you'd like more background, why not visit our conservatory at six-thirty? You could go now, but later there will be guides to explain things. Are you hungry?"

"No, we had a snack on the way down."

"Then if you don't mind waiting, why don't you join the campfire after conservatory? Most of our summer part-time help consists of high-school and college people, and they get together every Friday night.

"In fact, Ted," Mrs. Bowen went on, "you could be doing me quite a favor. I know something about your reputation, and you might be in a position to help me on this package matter. How about a quick tour of one of our other greenhouses, and then I will have to dash off for supper and freshen up for the conservatory."

They agreed to this as well, and stepped outside to wait for Mrs. Bowen while she made a telephone call.

"All right, Ted," said Nelson. "Let's put that analytical brain of yours to work and see what you can do to make some sense out of this."

"A special package arrived, was signed for by Mr. Gompers, taken to the office by Freddie Barker, and was missing when Miss Lance returned to the office some fifteen or twenty minutes later. Either Freddie or Miss Lance is lying, or else it was stolen during that period of time."

"I'm with you that far. If Freddie is lying I'll never believe anyone again."

"I agree. The most striking thing about this theft, it seems to me, is that it probably wasn't planned in advance. No one knew for sure the package would arrive today. Mr. Gompers couldn't have known that the truck driver would decide not to drive up the road to the office. It just happened that Freddie was on hand to carry the package up, and it was only chance that this all should have happened at a time when the office was temporarily empty. Someone just saw the opportunity, and decided to take advantage of it."

"What for, Ted? Mrs. Bowen didn't seem to think the cuttings would be of much use to anyone else."

"But they were of great use to her, and someone could have taken them with the idea of hurting her."

"What about the burglary of the office safe? How would that hurt her?"

"Well, since nothing was taken, it's possible that the thief was looking for something that wasn't there."

"I suppose it would have to be a thief. Only three persons knew the combination. Mr. and Mrs. Bowen could go into the safe any time they pleased, and Miss Lance was in there every day."

"It would have to be a very clever safecracker, unless—"

"—unless Miss Lance is lying," Nelson concluded. "But why should she claim the safe was entered if it wasn't? Mrs. Bowen places a lot of confidence in everybody, and this has all the earmarks of an inside job. How do you think the package was taken, Ted?"

"That fumigated greenhouse seems to cut off the rear pretty well. Even if a person could get through the locks, he would have trouble getting through that poisoned air."

Mrs. Bowen came out, and having locked up the office, was ready to take them for their greenhouse tour.

CHAPTER 3.

THE FUN HOUSE

MRS. Bowen opened the door and they followed her into the greenhouse. Although it had seemed long from outside, it seemed much longer down the aisles inside, for with the overflowing of greenery it was nearly impossible to see to the end. The entire building appeared to be about five-hundred feet long and three-hundred wide, and Ted, who liked to calculate such things in his head, figured that this would represent between three and four acres. A glass-paned wall reached up to the roof at each furrow, and separated the building into different rooms.

There was so much to see that they could hardly expect to grasp it all. Most of the working benches were table high, but some of the plots were close to the ground where more growing room was needed, and in some cases small pots were arranged on tiers.

There were side ventilators along the outer walls, some of them below the benches and others above, but the main ventilators were in the roof overhead, operated by a chain system. Looking upward, Nelson noticed a few panes missing.

"Yes, that's always a problem," Mrs. Bowen admitted when he pointed them out. "Frost breaks some of them; sometimes it is hail, especially if they are already cracked, and sometimes the putty works loose, or a ladder bumps them. If we can't think of anything else we blame sonic booms. I could use the services of a good glazier. Were you volunteering?"

"Are you serious?" Nelson inquired.

"Yes, I am," she said. "Have you had any previous experience?"

"Lots of it. I became an expert from kicking my football through the dining room window."

"Then I'm sure you'll be able to catch on quickly, though a somewhat different technique is used here. Can you begin tomorrow morning? I know you have a long drive, and if you like, you can spend the night in the cottage, at the opposite end of the estate."

"That sounds like a good deal. Is Ted invited, too?"

"Certainly, if he cares to stay. I think you'll find everything you need there. There's a large refrigerator in which I keep cold drinks for the workers, and there're always makings for sandwiches or snacks."

Ted agreed that he would stay, as long as he could get back to the office in the morning.

"Your roses surely have a lot of enemies, don't they?" asked Nelson as they walked along.

"Oh, yes, there are aphids and all kinds of beetles and harmful bees and budworms and earwigs and leafhoppers and midges and mites and scales and slugs and stem girdlers and thrips and mildew and nematodes—just to mention a few. I sometimes think it's a miracle that we are able to grow anything at all. When the soil gets too badly infested, we have to pasteurize it."

"Like milk?" asked Ted.

"A similar principle, yes."

As they turned a corner, they saw a slender, stooping man in coveralls approaching them. Seeing Mrs. Bowen, he took off his hat, and stepped aside for them to pass, but his employer paused to make introductions. After the men had shaken hands, Mrs. Bowen went on:

"Did you finish spraying the budding room, Mr. Thorton?"

"Yes, ma'am, I did, and right on schedule."

"What time were you out of there?"

"At three o'clock, ma'am, and not a minute after."

"And you bolted up the doors and locked the rear one?"

"I certainly did. I've got the key right here," and he patted his pocket, informing the visitors that there was only one key available, and here was the person responsible for it. "Is there anything wrong?"

"Nothing to do with the spraying. I'll talk to you later about it," and she nodded in dismissal.

At Mrs. Bowen's invitation, they stepped quickly through a doorway and closed the door behind them. This was the strangest room they had ever seen. It looked just like any of the other rooms, except for black panels instead of glass. Not a spark of daylight showed through; instead the lights were on.

"Our employees call this the Fun House," she explained. "Anyway, it's one of the rooms where we play tricks on our plants. Some plants have to be tricked into believing that the season is changing. We do this principally by varying the temperature or varying the light. We have these large ventilators in the roof, and if both the temperature and the lighting outside are satisfactory for our needs, we can open them. Otherwise we rely on artificial heating and cooling and lighting. Forget-me-nots are an example of a flower that grows best on an eight or ten-hour day, and should be in darkness the rest of the time. With 'mums it is even worse; 'mums won't bloom until the night is longer than the day. If you want them to bloom out of season, you can keep them in darkness for a longer time than the normal spring or summer night; if you want to delay their blooming, you turn on a light for a while during the night, and the plants will think the night still isn't long enough, and will refuse to bloom."

"Do you play these tricks on your roses?" Ted questioned.

"Not quite like this, for roses are harder to fool. You get them to bloom out of season by trying to duplicate the conditions of their best growing season, but you can't overwork them; they need their dormant season, too."

Leaving the Fun House, the visitors were shown into one of the most beautiful rooms they had ever seen. They recognized it at once as the orchid room.

"We never let the temperature here fall below sixty degrees," Mrs. Bowen explained, "and of course it is considerably warmer than that now. Besides warmth, orchids need good air circulation, light, high humidity, and lots of water that can drain off."

Nelson asked Mrs. Bowen if he could take a picture.

"Oh, do let me get cleaned up first," she objected.

Both Ted and Nelson thought a picture in her working clothes would be more effective for newspaper purposes, and she finally consented. Nelson snapped several pictures. Then, having shown them a telephone where they might call home, she left them.

At about six-thirty visitors began to arrive. Soon scores of people were wandering through the rose garden and the conservatory. Ted and Nelson joined them, and besides the wonderful display of flowers, speculated about the problems of setting up an accurate sundial squarely in the middle of the garden.

CHAPTER 4.

CAMPFIRE STORIES

AS twilight settled, the ranks of visitors gradually thinned out and finally dwindled into nothing. Most of the young people who worked on the estate had returned for the campfire which was soon blazing, and hamburgers, hot dogs and cheese were eaten in quantity.

If at first Ted and Nelson felt out of place, the feeling soon passed. These were all part-time workers, and some were not yet well acquainted with each other, but this hardly seemed to matter. Ted and Nelson met a girl called Tammi, who introduced them to the others. Freddie Barker was there, too, and said: "Listen, everybody, there was an important bundle taken out of the office this afternoon about three-thirty, or a little after. Did anybody happen to notice anything around that time?"

Most of the girls had been busy as hostesses at the afternoon conservatory, and the boys were scattered about the farm. Rolfe had been trimming the hedge in front, and remembered the arrival of the express truck, had seen Mr. Gompers sign for the bundle, and Freddie run up to the office with it.

"Did you notice any car pulling up to the office door?" Ted inquired.

"How about the back door?" someone asked.

"No, the greenhouse behind it had been fumigated, and all the doors were solidly bolted. That was completed around three o'clock."

"Oh, that's nonsense," said a girl named Laurel. "I saw Tony Thorton coming out of there after four."

"Are you sure you saw Mr. Thorton coming out at four o'clock?" asked Ted.

"It was after four. I know, because conservatory is over at four-thirty, and it was almost over then."

Although this contradicted what Mr. Thorton had said, Ted decided it wasn't very important—unless it was Tony Thorton who had stolen the package. Even if the fumigation had not been completed at three, and for some reason he wanted Mrs. Bowen to think it was, he at least must have been working in there at the time.

"About a car," said Rolfe slowly and thoughtfully. "There were so many cars coming and going on the drive that I didn't pay much attention. But it seems to me now that a car did drive past the parking lot and pull up in front of the office door."

"Was that soon after the arrival of the express truck?"

"I guess it was, but I'm kind of hazy about it."

"What kind of car was it?"

"A big shiny red convertible," and he added with a laugh, "probably a Chrysler Imperial."

"If there's a car like that in the neighborhood it shouldn't be too hard to find," Nelson offered.

But Tammi said, "That's just a joke. Chrysler Imperial is the name of a prize-winning rose."

"Did you notice how long the car stopped?" Ted went on.

"Only a minute or two, I guess, but I wasn't paying much attention. I had other things on my mind: hedges, hostesses, and home."

"Miss Lance's boy friend often comes to pick her up," someone suggested.

"No, he drives a green roadster," said Rolfe, and Ted and Nelson could confirm this.

No one else had noticed the car, but considering the flow of visitors, that was not unusual, nor could Rolfe offer any further clues. The others asked a few questions about the missing bundle, and then the conversation drifted into other channels.

"If he was joking about the Chrysler Imperial," said Nelson to Tammi, "do you think he really saw a car or is the whole thing a joke?"

"He must have seen a car, and it was probably a red convertible, but I don't think he has any idea what kind it was."

"What color is a Chrysler Imperial rose?"

"It's called an oxblood red, and it's a hybrid tea about medium height, with a pleasant fragrance. I don't think there are any in the garden, though Mrs. B. probably has some in the greenhouses."

"What does a rose need to be patentable?" asked Ted curiously.

"Well, it must be a *new* rose; that is, there must be some feature about it that is distinctively different from any other rose that has been on sale or described in print in the United States or abroad, and it must breed true to form from cuttings. You have a year to apply for your patent; after that it would be too late."

Nelson was puzzled. "I suppose it is illegal to take a cutting from a patented rose without permission, but what if you crossed your own roses and happened to get something just like a rose that was patented?"

"Well, of course, just like an invention, the one who gets the patent first would be the one to own it. But the patent-holder might have a fight on his hands to prove that the second rose was so much like his own that it shouldn't be sold."

"Is the Loki Pageant of Roses important?" Ted inquired.

"It's a good one, and has a lot of tradition back of it. It would certainly be a good first step. I understand Mrs. B. intends to enter Governor Hope this year. None of us has seen it yet, but we're all very curious and excited."

So Governor Hope was a secret, and at the same time not a secret. Probably Mrs. Bowen had not been able to reach a decision about it until a couple of weeks ago when she saw how it was blooming. Very likely she had only a few plants, and if things turned out favorably at Loki, she would patent it and go into commercial production of it next year. There would be no point in publicizing it too much before the Loki show.

"Is Tammi your real name or a nickname?" Nelson asked.

She grimaced. "If I told you the real story you might not believe it. Yes, Tammi is my real name, but people are always asking me if it's a nickname, so once I told my high-school friends it was short for Tambourine. And what happened after that is too horrible to tell. Somehow that name got on my high-school records, and my high-school diploma was made out to Tambourine, and when I applied for admission to college all my credits were in that name. It would have been so confusing to change it that I let it stand, and now it looks as though I'm named Tambourine for the rest of my life!"

"Let's tell ghost stories," a boy suggested to the group.

"Tammi first," someone said, since she had let it be known she had a story ready.

"You may find it hard to believe this," she began, "but it happened here just this week. It was after conservatory, and it seemed that the visitors were slower going home than usual. Although it was late, I still had a little longer to wait for my ride home, so I was standing here by myself, looking out toward the fir trees.

"Suddenly I saw a wolf come leaping through the trees. I was petrified, but he wasn't paying any attention to me. He ran across the field and leaped that little hedge over there. I stood there watching, wondering if I was seeing things. I waited for him to come out, but he didn't. Instead, it was a man who came out, pushing through the hedge. He walked over toward the greenhouse, and walked right *through the wall,* then made his way down the aisle. I wanted to scream, but I thought that this might only make him come after me, and there wasn't anyone near to help. Then I thought that probably I was only dreaming anyway, so what was the use of being scared?

"As I stood there, he came back up the aisle, and he walked *right through* the wall again. He went over to the hedge and pushed through it, and a moment later a wolf leaped over the hedge and went bounding across the field and through the fir trees, and I could hear him baying down in the swamp.

"I'd had enough, and I ran back to the road, where my father had just pulled up. I asked him if he had heard anything, and he said no, so I didn't have the nerve to tell him what I had seen. If I had, he would have wanted to go after it, and I didn't want him to, so I didn't say anything more."

"A werewolf?" someone asked. "A man that changes into a wolf, and back?"

"How could you see him in the greenhouse?" a boy objected. "Was he carrying a light?"

"No, I don't think so."

"Well, there wasn't any moon that night. There's only a little dinky moon tonight."

"Anyway, it *seemed* as though I could see him. I can't explain it."

"What's beyond that little hedge?" asked Nelson.

"Nothing. It's just a little space for rubbish cans and things like that, and the hedge is in front so it won't look unsightly."

"A real good story, Tammi," said Ted, as the party broke up. "How much of it did you make up?"

She turned toward him, her eyes wide and bright in the moonlight. "I didn't make up any of it, Ted. I told it exactly the way I saw it."

CHAPTER 5.

DO WEREWOLVES EAT SALAMI?

THE cottage, normally locked at night, had been left open for them. There were just two rooms, a large kitchen, including a refrigerator and stove, and a bedroom. Although the bunk beds were not made up, there was bed linen available, and towels, and coveralls for working clothes.

"You can't be hungry already," Ted remarked, as Nelson opened the refrigerator door and examined its contents carefully.

"Just checking on breakfast," his friend replied, shutting the door. "How'd you like Tammi's yarn?"

"Oh, I don't doubt that she can make up a pretty good story."

"But the way she stuck to it. I don't dig her yet. I'm not very sleepy. Want to do a little checking up on her?"

"Like what?"

"Like looking over the locale. Admit it, Ted—there's monkey business of some sort going on around here."

They had no trouble at all finding the hedge and the little space that it concealed. Their information was correct: it led nowhere, and unless one had rubbish to dump, or tools or a wheelbarrow to put out of the way, there would be no purpose in going there—unless you needed a hiding place.

The moon had set, and the fir trees waved against a black sky, and the stillness of the country had settled over them like a shroud.

"Tammi *did* see something," Nelson asserted. "She didn't make up that story out of whole cloth. It would make it a lot easier if she would tell us exactly what she saw."

"But that's what she claims she did," Ted reminded him.

"I remember a story I read about the way hungry wolves will begin to run in a circle until the weakest member falls, and then they pounce on him and eat him."

Another part of Tammi's story seemed to check out, too. As they tried to trace the path the intruder would have taken from the hedge to the greenhouse, they saw that indeed there were no doors anywhere around. If he had entered the greenhouse, he must have walked through the glass-paned wall. And it did seem, if there was a trace of twilight still in the sky, that she might have been able to see someone inside the greenhouse, making his way down the aisle.

"And don't forget, Ted, Miss Lance still believes that someone went into the safe. This might be the agent responsible, who was looking for something."

"What was he looking for, a bone?"

They retraced their steps across the field to the far hedge, where the wolf had allegedly disappeared through the fir trees. When they had passed beneath the trees, it seemed that they had entered a different world. The greenhouses and cultivated fields were behind them, and in front lay a primitive desolation of marshland, trees, and a few uncertain paths. They had no intention of going any further that night.

"Pretty swampy," said Nelson. "Might be quicksand, too. You could easily get lost in there and maybe step into some mire so that they'd never even find your social security card."

Then out of the impenetrable darkness in front of them there came a mournful baying. So sudden and unexpected was the sound, so much did it contrast with the country stillness, that they stood frozen and momentarily stunned.

"A-a *real* wolf?" Nelson asked in a whisper when he had regained his voice.

"I don't know. Sounds like it could be. How can you tell? That's the river down there, isn't it, and it wanders down from the hills. I've heard of an occasional deer around. Maybe a wolf could have worked his way down here."

"Maybe not a wolf, Ted, but something just as bad—a dog that has gone wild. That happens every once in a while. A wolf is at least predictable, but I'd hate to meet up with a wild dog that didn't know which side of civilization it was on. Want to get back?"

"May as well. My feet are getting cold."

They did not hear the sound again, but it was only by a strong act of will that they refrained from looking over their shoulders as they walked back to the cottage. They no longer doubted that Tammi had seen . . . something . . . and there was no way of doubting that they had heard . . . something. It could easily have been the same thing.

By the time they were ready for bed and about to switch off the light, having previously made sure all the windows were locked and the doors bolted, Nelson's common sense was pushing to the fore.

"Let's be reasonable about this, Ted. What's across the river? Probably some farms, right? And a farmer might have a dog tied out, and the dog might get lonesome and start howling, right? I noticed the wind was from that direction. That might be all there was to what we heard."

Ted nodded agreement.

"All right so far," Nelson went on. "Now Tammi's story. Maybe she didn't see anything at all. Maybe she saw a neighborhood dog running around, and her imagination turned it into a wolf. Then she sees, or thinks she sees, a wolf turn into a man. Well, I don't care if it's a wolf or a werewolf or a man, nothing can walk right through a wall, so she has to be wrong. Probably the moonlight was playing tricks on her."

"There wasn't any moon," Ted pointed out.

"So maybe the tricks were all inside her head. And as for somebody going into the safe, if somebody did, that was almost certainly an inside job, right?"

"Right," said Ted, with a little more enthusiasm.

"So then why don't we forget about it and turn out the light and go to sleep?"

"All right by me, if you can sleep with the windows closed."

When Ted awakened he found that Nelson was already stirring around. He seemed to have lost his determination to believe everything was all right, and was moody once more. But he said nothing until Ted was washed, dressed, and ready to face the world.

"I think I can stand it now," said Ted cheerfully.

"No, don't stand it. Sit down. Ted, I'll give it to you straight. Somebody broke in here last night!"

"What!"

Nelson nodded. "I woke up during the night and thought I heard a noise. Somebody was in the kitchen."

"Well, why didn't you wake me up?" Ted demanded.

"What for? If there's a burglar in the house the best thing you can do is stay asleep. After a while when I didn't hear anything more, I thought he must be gone, so I got up and moseyed around and looked out the windows, but I couldn't see anything."

"Is anything of yours missing?"

"Yes and no. That package of salami is missing from the refrigerator. Well, what's so funny about that?" he demanded indignantly as Ted exploded into laughter. "Don't you think I know whether or not the salami is missing? It isn't so important what's missing, as the fact that somebody broke in."

"All right, Nel," said Ted. "You checked the refrigerator last night, and then we went out to look over the grounds. We didn't lock up the place, and we couldn't if we wanted to, because we don't have a key. You didn't check the refrigerator when we came back, did you?"

"Well, no," Nelson admitted lamely.

"So if the salami is missing, it was probably taken while the place was wide open."

"We left a light on," Nelson reminded him. "It would take a bold thief to walk into a place that might be occupied with people still up and awake."

"Not if he saw us leave. He might have realized the place was empty."

"Well, all right, Ted, but I don't like it, anyway. What's somebody doing hanging around here? And what about that noise I heard in the night?"

"You aren't sure it came from inside the house, are you?"

Nelson considered. "No, but it sure sounded like it."

"Well, what sort of thief would that be? If he knew the place was occupied, I don't think he would have broken in just for some salami. If he didn't think it was occupied, why should he have been so quiet that you aren't even sure you heard him? What about the doors and windows?"

"Everything still snug and tight," Nelson said, shaking his head. "I checked them carefully just before you got up."

"All right, then. The doors were bolted, so a key wouldn't have helped an intruder any, and the windows are still latched. You want to admit nobody broke in last night?"

"You sure make it sound awfully logical, Ted. You've almost convinced me that I didn't hear what I heard. Want any breakfast?"

"Let's go out and eat. I wonder if werewolves eat salami?"

"I think you're getting a big charge out of this, Ted."

"I admit I wouldn't mind seeing a werewolf, but I don't ever expect to be that lucky."

"Werewolf or not, there are a lot of things around here that need explaining."

Nelson was busy putting his effects together, and he even threw a pair of coveralls over his arm so that he wouldn't have to return to the cottage later. Obviously he had had enough of the place.

They found a little roadside place for breakfast. Nelson wanted Ted to take his car to drive home, coming out later in the day to pick him up. But Ted was uncertain how much work awaited him at the office, and decided to take the bus instead. He arrived at the *Town Crier* office to find that he was faced with a busy day. Mr. Dobson questioned him about his interview with Mrs. Bowen, and then decided that this would make a good background story for the upcoming pageant.

"Make it twelve inches, Ted."

Mr. Dobson was too busy just then to listen to yarns told around a campfire about a farm dog that howled from across the river, and a hungry tramp who walked off with a package of salami, and a safe that *might* have been entered but not rifled, and a pilfered package that would be of no use to the thief. All these things had nothing to do with the story that Ted had been sent to get, so he decided to say nothing for the present. At the same time he was more than a little anxious to get back to the Lady Bee Floral Nursery again. These things intrigued him, and though any one of these mischances was perhaps of little significance, Ted wondered whether, in total, they might be adding up to something sinister.

Nelson drove up in front of Ted's home a little after six.

"Anything doing, Ted?"

"More work for you. Mr. Dobson wants me to interview a few of the local flower growers. I was pretty busy today, and anyway I thought it might be just as well to wait for your camera. Put in a good day?"

"You bet, in more ways than one. Climbing around those green-house roofs is *fun.*"

"Wasn't it hot?"

"Oh, I worked mostly on the shady side. And I picked up lots of news, too."

"For instance?"

"Item One. Guess where Mr. Bowen is spending the weekend?"

"How should I know?"

"In the clink! Yes, that's right, he's in the town jail in Holiday. He called up while I was there, and as long as I heard that much, Mrs. B. told me the rest."

"What's he in jail for?"

"For digging up a wild rose on public property. I understand it's kind of an obsession with rose-fanciers, something they just can't resist. It isn't just that the rose is pretty, but that they always imagine it might have some important chromosomes or genes that they can cross with something else and come up with a perfect rose. Of course they wouldn't steal a rose from private property, and they certainly wouldn't dig up a rose in a public park. But there's a lot of abandoned land around that doesn't seem to belong to anybody, and then they sometimes take a chance."

"What about bail?"

"He said it's Saturday, and there doesn't seem to be anybody around with authority to release him. He doesn't mind—says he's got some books with him and it will give him a chance to catch up. And Mrs. B. is philosophical about it. She said she always knew it would happen someday.

"Item Two. I saw Tammi for a few minutes at the afternoon conservatory and asked her about her werewolf story. Every thing came out just the same way it did before. She said it spoils a ghost story to change it. I still don't have her figured."

Ted nodded, and Nelson continued: "Item Three. I really do think there is some prowler walking through those greenhouses at night, Ted. I overheard Mr. Gompers talking about it a little, and he thinks he's seen someone. I also found out that the greenhouses have a burglar alarm system. You can't go through a door after dark without sounding an alarm—unless you know how to short out the system, and nobody has ever done that. But I've been thinking that a greenhouse must be just about the hardest place in the world to keep somebody out of. All you've got to do is cut out a pane of glass somewhere. The panes are sixteen by twenty, and most men could squeeze through them if they wanted to."

"Did you find any empty panes?"

"Oh, sure. There're always broken windows around a greenhouse. I was looking right at a frame that I thought must have a particularly clean pane of glass. Then I put my hand through the frame, and it was empty.

"Item Four. There are no farms across the river; anyway, not right across. It's kind of wooded and desolate. Whatever we heard was out in the woods there somewhere, on one side of the river or the other. Anyway I'm glad I'm not spending the night alone in that cottage.

"And Item Five. . . ." He paused, and Ted wondered if he had saved the most important thing to last.

"I think I've seen our Chrysler Imperial, Ted, and furthermore, I've got the license number."

CHAPTER 6.

BLUE LADY

TED stared at him. "What's this stuff about Chrysler Imperial? Tammi said it was just a joke, and Rolfe admitted he didn't see the car closely enough to tell."

"Rolfe saw the car and gave a description of it—and then added maybe it was a Chrysler Imperial," said Nelson. "But something about the car must have suggested Chrysler Imperial to him, or at least it could have been one."

"I agree that it *could* have been a Chrysler Imperial. Then what?"

"Well, I ran a couple of errands today for Mrs. B. in her pick-up, and when I ran into a station for gas, what do you think I saw sitting there? A great big, new, shiny, red Chrysler Imperial. That's when bells started to ring. I didn't see the driver; he was in the car just pulling out. But I did have time to get the license number. *Now* what do you think, Ted?"

Ted considered the matter carefully. "Of course the car fits the description Rolfe gave, even apart from the make, and we've located it in the right area. Still, you might be able to find at least half a dozen other cars like that in the neighborhood."

"You've got an in with Sergeant Jeffers. There'd be no trouble at all identifying the owner of the car through the license number. Maybe the name would be somebody we recognized."

"And if it wasn't, then what?"

"It wouldn't hurt for you to talk to the driver, would it?"

"It's possible that if he was the one who entered the office, he might have noticed something, even if he wasn't the one who stole the bundle of clippings."

"And it's also possible he's the thief, because we haven't been able to pinpoint anyone else on the scene. But maybe you know more about the laws of slander than I do. I know you wouldn't make any accusations you couldn't back up, but some people are touchy about insinuations, too."

"I thought you were eager to talk to him a moment ago," Ted chided.

"I was eager for *you* to talk to him." Nelson grinned.

But their newspaper assignment came first. Nelson was back after eating and washing up. He had both cameras with him.

"I'm not going to get caught again without a colored film, when I'm talking to people who raise flowers. I'm going to take at least two or three rolls with me next week out to Lady Bee's—if I don't break my fool neck first on those glazing ladders."

At their first stop, the people were not at home, and though they could see the garden from the front of the house, they decided not to investigate further. They went on to the home of Mr. and Mrs. King, and the couple came out to greet them and show them the garden.

Since Ted was interested in talking, and Nelson in taking pictures, the group seemed to break up naturally with Ted and Mrs. King in one part, Mr. King and Nelson in the other. At least Ted's experience now enabled him to talk more intelligently about roses than he could the day before, and consequently he was more at ease.

"Many of my plants come from the Lady Bee Nursery," said Mrs. King, when Ted mentioned his visit there the previous day. "They are well known for their integrity. This is the first time I have ever tried to show any of my roses, and I suppose it seems presumptuous to believe I would have any chance against such a commercial producer as Mrs. Bowen, with so many more plants to choose from."

"I'm afraid I don't know nearly as much about roses as I'd like to," Ted said, "but yours seem very nice to me. Which ones were you planning to enter?"

She hesitated. "It's a little early to say for sure. The judging takes place Thursday evening, and that's five days away. It's hard to be sure just which one will reach the peak of perfection at that time. Here is one I'd like to enter in the hybrid tea lavender class. I call it Blue Lady."

She led him to a bush that obviously was the apple of her eye. In spite of the name, the rose was a nearly pure lavender—though perhaps rose breeders always live in hopes of a perfect blue rose. The shade was most unusual, Ted thought, but whether that was a good thing or not he didn't know. It might be unusual simply because most people didn't care for it. It did take a little bit of getting used to, especially if a person liked red roses, and the redder the better. Certainly Blue Lady didn't shout at you; it seemed much too delicate and refined for that.

"I'm sure a good deal must depend on the preference of the judges," he remarked.

"Yes, it does, and that is why I never feel disappointed about losing."

"Can you tell me something about how roses are judged?"

"They use a point system. Form and color count twenty-five points apiece, substance and foliage are twenty points apiece, and size is ten points. In England, I understand, they prefer larger flowers, while they hardly consider the foliage at all. The English also like their show flowers more fully open than is customary in America."

She seemed to be waiting for him to say something more, and he hardly knew what sort of encouragement to give her. Obviously, the Governor Hope rose wasn't going to have the lavender class to itself, nor could such a thing be expected. In that case there would be no reason for holding a contest.

"I certainly hope you do enter Blue Lady, Mrs. King. Since it is in the lavender class, it ought to have a good chance against other roses in the same class, even if the judges don't particularly care for lavender."

"Yes, though of course you always do have some hope for a Queen of the Show award."

"Where did you get Blue Lady? Is it a standard variety?"

"No, as far as I know I made up the name myself. It was a gift from my sister, who brought it back from a trip to the West Coast. She's not much of a rose fancier herself, and I had little hope for it. I supposed it was probably a variety that was used to the warmer climate out there, and might not do at all well here. But to my surprise it turned out very well. This was the first year it bloomed, and I was startled at the shade. I called up my sister to congratulate her on her good taste, but she said it was just luck."

Nelson took pictures of Mr. and Mrs. King for the *Town Crier,* and a number of colored pictures for himself. He didn't need Ted to ask him to include Blue Lady among that number.

They had one more call to make, and Mrs. Arthur's garden proved both smaller than the Kings' and less selective. Their hostess readily admitted as much. They talked to her briefly, took some pictures and left.

"Now the police station," Nelson reminded Ted.

Ted could see no objection. At the station Sergeant Jeffers was glad to oblige them, as soon as he had a free moment. He knew that Ted, as a newspaper reporter, was entitled to such information. He gave them a name and address written on a piece of paper.

Outside the station they looked at the paper. The name, Fritz Glick, meant nothing at all to Nelson, much to his disappointment. He was quite sure it was not the name of anyone employed at Lady Bee's.

"You didn't expect it, did you?" Ted asked. "You didn't spot that car in the parking lot."

Nelson was still studying the card, trying to figure out the address, which was given as a route number.

"I think it must be about twenty-five or thirty miles from here. Want to take a ride?"

"Tonight? What's the rush, and do you think it would do any good?"

"It might, and we might as well check it out now as any other time."

"Well, let's think it out first. According to the address, he must live at least fifty miles from Lady Bee's, so what would he be doing stopping at a service station in Lutz?" (Lutz was the small town a few miles from the nursery.) "The most likely thing is that he was just passing through on a trip, found his gas running low, and stopped at a handy station. If that's what happened on Saturday, it isn't likely he was out there on Friday afternoon. What's your theory?"

"My idea is that he probably works in Lutz, or someplace nearby. I know Lutz isn't much of a place, but it does have a few businesses. Fifty miles isn't a long distance to commute. Maybe it's a special kind of job, the kind he likes, or maybe it's only a temporary job, or maybe he's planning to move closer to his work when he can."

"As long as he doesn't work at the nursery, he wouldn't have any chance of knowing about the bundle."

"No, we agreed that whoever took the bundle probably did it on the spur of the moment. He might have had some business at the greenhouse—maybe wanted to buy some plants—saw the bundle and helped himself. It could even be a mistake: he was instructed to pick up a package, thought that was it, and left." Nelson paused. "The more I think about it, I'll bet that's just what happened. Otherwise why steal something that isn't of any value to you?"

"Then why didn't he return it when he found out his mistake?"

"Maybe he hasn't found out his mistake yet."

"So that's the story you want me to try out on Fritz Glick when we call on him?"

"What do you mean?" asked Nelson, stung. "I really believe it."

In the end Ted allowed himself to be persuaded. They drove out to the house, and a young man answered their ring.

"Well?"

"I'm Ted Wilford, and this is Nelson Morgan."

"Wonderful! I've been waiting all my life to meet you. What magazines are you selling?"

"We're not selling anything. We just wondered if you were the owner of a Chrysler Imperial?"

"You know darn well that I am, or you wouldn't ask. What about it?"

"It's a little complicated. Do you mind if we come in and talk about it?"

"Rather. We'll stand out here and talk." Glick came out on the porch and closed the door firmly behind him. There were chairs on the porch, but they were not invited to sit down.

"We're trying to trace a Chrysler Imperial that was seen near Lady Bee's yesterday afternoon. We're not sure that it's yours, but thought it might be."

"And suppose it isn't?"

"In that case we don't have anything to talk to you about," said Ted evenly.

Glick nodded cynically. "I get it now. There's been some sort of accident, and you've got a description of the car, and now you want me to tell you if I'm the guilty party. Well, I'm sorry to disappoint you, but I haven't run over anybody's dog this year."

"It isn't like that at all," Nelson broke in, forgetting his resolution to let Ted do the talking. "There was a bundle taken, probably by mistake, and we were wondering if you might have picked up the wrong package."

"I see." He turned his scowling face upon Nelson. "And I suppose you've got this other bundle with you, all ready to make the exchange."

"Well, no," Nelson admitted, having failed to foresee this weak point in his story.

"Just what was in this bundle anyway?"

"What difference does it make to you, as long as you don't have it?"

"I suppose you were working Friday afternoon?" asked Ted mildly.

"Naturally. Do I look like the U.S. mint? And if you want to know where I was working, you'll have to find out from somebody besides me. Furthermore, just for your information, I couldn't have been driving my car Friday afternoon even if I wanted to. It was in a garage."

"Trouble with a new car like that already?" Nelson demanded.

"No accident, if that's what you're thinking. I just happen to be fussy about my cars, and when something isn't exactly right, I want it corrected pronto. Now will you excuse me? I've got a date, and I don't think I want you two phonies along. You'd do better selling magazines."

Glick waited till they were in their car before going inside.

"Well, Ted, was he right? Were we phonies?"

"I don't think so. It's always permissible to make inquiries when you're on legitimate business. And you told him the truth, or what you thought was the truth, but he wouldn't believe you. He had his own ideas. We found out something. He didn't deny being near Lutz Friday afternoon, which he easily could have, if that means anything. I'm beginning to think maybe you're right—he does work in or near Lutz. If it's true that his car was in a garage, that wouldn't be hard to check out. There probably isn't more than one in Lutz."

"Probably the station where I saw him gassing up today. So we've come around in a circle right back to where we started."

"We're a little bit better off. If the car was in the station on Friday, he couldn't have used it. But someone at the station could."

CHAPTER 7.

A DANGEROUS THEFT

LATE Sunday evening Nelson packed his suitcase with some reluctance.

"There's no use commuting a hundred-fifty miles every day, when Mrs. B. is willing for me to stay at the cottage. Would, ah, you like to come out and spend the night there, Ted?"

"Then I'd be commuting, wouldn't I? It hardly seems worth it on the chance of seeing a salami-eating werewolf. Just make sure there's plenty of meat in the refrigerator, and probably he won't bother you at all."

But gloomy Nelson wasn't going to be kidded into good humor, and said, as Ted was about to leave, "I'll keep in touch with you, and let you know about anything strange going on. I don't think we're at the end of things yet. Don't you think Tammi's a pretty nice girl?"

"Truthfully, I hadn't given the matter a whole lot of thought."

"Well, do," and evidently he hoped this would be an added inducement for Ted to come to Lady Bee's. Ted would have been more than willing, for any sort of mystery attracted him like a magnet, but he was supposed to be working for the *Town Crier,* and he could hardly justify a stay at the cottage as representing business.

The hardworking newspaper staff met their noon deadline for the issue that would be out early the next morning, but there was little time to relax, for they began to plan promptly for the Friday issue. Mr. Dobson intended to feature the Loki Pageant of Roses which would be in full swing by that time. Unfortunately, the judging on Thursday evening would be too late for the Friday edition, and they would have to resort to a pretense of being right up to date when actually they were unavoidably in arrears. By knowing what was going to be entered, by talking to many of the people concerned, they might be able to draw a fairly accurate picture of what was to come, except that they would never dare actually to predict the winners.

Ted's interview with Mrs. Bowen, and her picture, were already on the presses, as well as a brief story about some of the contestants he had talked with. But the pictures of the local participants had been deferred to the next issue, which would have a special two-page spread. There would be a picture of Governor Hope, too, who had promised to attend the pageant, and the item that Mrs. Bowen had named a rose after him was being withheld until that time.

Late in the afternoon the call from Nelson came. It was far from a routine call, and Nelson sounded keyed up.

"You'd better get down here fast, Ted. Something more's been taken and it's nothing little this time."

"Something valuable?"

"Not valuable but dangerous. You may have a real newspaper story. I can't talk now. See you," and he hung up abruptly.

Ted smiled as he replaced the receiver. He had no doubt at all that Nelson was pressed for time. But he also knew him well enough to feel sure that Nelson was trying to get him to come down.

There was nothing to do except lay the whole matter in front of Mr. Dobson, who also smiled, for he, too, knew Nelson.

"I can see why Nelson's anxious for your company, Ted, but nevertheless I trust his judgment. If he says this present matter is important, then I'm very sure it is. All these previous things, while suggestive, didn't add up to enough, but if matters have now taken a sinister turn, I think you'd better get down there."

"I'm on my way."

"Want to take my car?"

"No, I think the bus will be handy enough. I don't imagine things are quite that urgent. How long do I have down there?"

"Use your own judgment entirely, Ted. Call in from time to time and let me know how you're making out."

At home Ted made brief explanations to his mother, who insisted that he eat while she packed his suitcase for him.

"How long will you be gone, Ted?"

"No telling, Mom, but give me enough for a week. Are you planning on attending the Loki show?"

"I wouldn't miss it, Ted. Although I'm not a member of the garden club, I've attended several meetings as a guest, and I know how much their hearts are set on it. Do you expect Mrs. Bowen's Governor Hope rose to win?"

"I don't know. I haven't seen it yet. But I know how much she is hoping for it. I suppose you'd feel sort of funny, naming a rose after the governor, and then it turns out not to be much of a rose after all."

By eight o'clock he was at Lady Bee's. It was the evening conservatory hour, and visitors were numerous. Nelson must have kept one eye on the road, for he was there to meet him.

"All right, Nel, let me have it," Ted commanded. "What was stolen?"

Nelson eyed Ted's packed suitcase with satisfaction, and plunged right in. "A tank of poison spray!"

"Poison?" Ted frowned, trying to figure out just how important such a theft might be. Certainly such poisons were quite numerous, and he didn't feel that they were particularly difficult to procure.

"Don't make any mistake about it, Ted," said Nelson. "This stuffs deadly. It doesn't hurt you if you're alert, because it makes your eyes smart and you choke a little and you get out of there fast. But suppose a person was breathing it under circumstances where he couldn't get away. In about ten minutes it would be just too bad."

"Why would a person steal it? Couldn't he purchase it somewhere?"

"Sure he could, if he wants to let everybody know he's got it, and take out a license and sign a purchase form. That's the whole thing. Anybody who wants to use it legitimately can get it. The only reason to steal it would be if he intended to use it in some other way."

"What does Mrs. B. think about it?"

"She thinks it's the work of juveniles and that they may have taken something deadly without realizing just how dangerous it is. That's the theory she gave to the police."

"And what do they think?"

"They're not buying it for a minute. Come along, and I'll show you why."

He led the way to the strong room, at the west end of one of the greenhouses. The police had completed their investigation and left. The room was of solid stone, with a good foundation and no windows. The only opening was a door, solidly padlocked, or rather, double-padlocked. One padlock used a key, the other a combination. Most remarkable of all, nothing seemed to have been disturbed. Conceivably the door could have been smashed in, or a tunnel dug underneath and the concrete floor broken through, but no such thing had happened.

"If it was juveniles who did that, they're past the reform-school stage. They're all ready for Leavenworth."

"You'd sure think so," Ted agreed. "Well, who's the custodian of the keys?"

"That's where the thing rubs, Ted. Mr. and Mrs. Bowen and Mr. Gompers all knew the combination, but only Mr. Gompers had a key. It's another one of those situations where the Bowens didn't want a lot of keys floating around. They wanted just one key, and one man responsible for it."

"And how did Mr. Gompers react to that?"

"I thought he had a lot of poise, but this thing almost knocked him off his underpins. When the police questioned him he stammered and flushed and sweated and finally shouted. If he'd been the culprit he would have been able to carry it off a little better than that. One thing's for sure: he never took it."

"Unless he has a flair for dramatics. But you're probably right. Why should he steal in such a way that the finger of guilt was certain to point directly at him? Any chance that the door was accidentally left open?"

"He claims not. The rules about it are very strict: open the door, go in and get what you want, then lock the door immediately. If he did leave it open, the blame would still fall on him, so maybe that helped upset him. But that wouldn't be as bad as stealing the stuff himself, so he could have tried to take that way out. But he didn't."

"Who discovered the theft?"

"They take inventory every few days. Mrs. B. was with him, and he opened the door. They missed it at once. Well, what do you make of it?"

"Obviously Mr. Gompers was the only one who could have taken it, and obviously he didn't take it. So that leaves us in the middle of nowhere."

"Ted," said Nelson thoughtfully, "you know you always say: when several unusual things happen together, there's a chance they're all connected. Well, look at all the things that have happened before this theft: a prowler in the greenhouses, somebody's entering the safe, the missing bundle of clippings, Tammi's werewolf, the howling from the swamp, the theft of the salami at the cottage—how do you connect everything up?"

Ted considered carefully for a minute or two. "The salami was probably taken by a hungry tramp who happened past—or less likely, maybe one of the kids came for it after the campfire. I don't put that in a class with the other things. We've got three cases of breaking and entering: the greenhouses, the office safe, and the strong room of poisons. I think anybody could break into the greenhouses who knew enough about how the burglar alarms were set, but the other two suggest some high-class work.

"Then there are two cases of theft: the bundle of clippings and the poison tank. The bundle might possibly be of use to someone, so that could be robbery for gain. But the poison isn't of much use to anyone unless he intends to commit another crime. Here again we haven't any idea what sort of crime it would be, except that it would have to be a violent one. A crime for gain and a crime of violence seem to me to be exact opposites. I can't picture the same person doing both things unless—"

"Unless what, Ted?" asked Nelson as he paused.

"Well, let's say that there was no profit in stealing the bundle and no profit in stealing the poison and no further crime intended. The purpose of the thefts could be to discredit Mrs. B. somehow."

"How could those things discredit her?"

"I can't very well think how. The theft of the bundle wasn't even reported to the police, I suppose. The theft of the poison could get her in bad with the police, I imagine, if they thought she was being careless about poisons. They might even cancel her license, and that could hurt."

Nelson was dubious. "That sounds awfully far-fetched to me, Ted."

"It does to me, too. I wonder if possibly everything that's happened is a diversion of some sort. We've been so busy looking at all these things around the edge that we don't see what's happening in the middle."

"It is a puzzle, isn't it?" said a new voice, and a man Ted didn't know stepped up to join them.

"Oh, Mr. Bowen." Nelson recognized him, and introduced him to Ted.

"Yes, I've heard that you boys have been around during my absence," said Mr. Bowen, shaking hands. "Well, it's good to get home again, I guess, even if there is a tankful of poisonous gas floating around somewhere. My jail cell was comfortable, but rather confining."

"Did they let you keep your rose bush?" asked Nelson, who, having met Mr. Bowen before, felt he could be a little freer with him.

"No, worse luck. They made me plant it again, then let me off with a warning and court costs. Oh, well, it probably wasn't anything anyway, but you always hope."

"Can't you go back for a clipping?"

"No chance. I think they've got me spotted by now. Want to walk back to the office with me? I've got a few things to ask you. My wife said she heard something about stories the kids were telling around the campfire. Is there anything in that?"

Between them they told the story of Tammi's werewolf. Mr. Bowen seemed unimpressed. "I've noticed before that Tambourine has quite an imagination."

The name startled them both, and they looked at each other with amusement, but made no comment.

"By the way, we're going to make a big search of the place for that tank tomorrow. The police asked us to, for they don't have the manpower to do the job themselves."

"Wouldn't the thief have taken the tank off by now?" Ted queried.

"Maybe not. If it was stolen in the daytime, he might have had trouble getting very far with it without being observed."

"Isn't it more likely it was stolen at night?"

"I'd suppose so, if I could figure out how it was stolen at all. But there you have the additional problem of the burglar alarm. It goes on automatically when the rest of the alarm system is set, and nothing in the system was disturbed. I suppose there's no harm in telling you that the alarm system is set from our home, over there." He nodded toward a house adjoining the estate. "To shut off the alarm system, a burglar would first have to break into our home, and that in itself would create an alarm. Cutting the wire to the greenhouses won't help, because that is one of the very things which touches off the alarm."

Conservatory was over, and the visitors were leaving. Mrs. Bowen was talking to a small group, and when they left she walked over to the office.

"Come on along, boys," Mr. Bowen invited. "My wife wanted to ask you about your newspaper story, Ted. Will it be in tomorrow, and will you get her a copy?"

Ted nodded, but had no chance to say anything further, as they stepped into the office. Mr. Gompers was there waiting for Mrs. Bowen, and he was in an angry mood again, while his employer tried to be soothing. They heard her say:

"I certainly didn't intend to accuse you of anything, Mr. Gompers. It's just that I don't understand some of these entries, and I thought perhaps you could explain."

"Of course you don't understand them. I don't understand them myself. They are obvious forgeries. Can't you see what's going on here? Somebody is trying to throw everything my way."

CHAPTER 8.

THE ALLEGED FORGERIES

THEN Mrs. Bowen and Mr. Gompers noticed the arrival of the others.

"What's the trouble?" asked Mr. Bowen, while the two boys wondered if they were expected to leave.

"It's some of the entries in our daybook. Mr. Gompers claims they are forgeries. Of course I'm not doubting his word, if he is really sure, but I just can't imagine why anybody would forge such a thing." She went on to explain to Ted and Nelson, as though perhaps they could throw some light on the matter. "This is a record of our daily working schedules, what we did, and so on. The particular thing which Mr. Gompers claims is forged is some of the entries having to do with hybrids, just which kind of crosses we made on special varieties of roses."

"Well, it's more important to figure out first what happened," Mr. Bowen observed. "After that we can try to figure out why it happened. Now just which sheets do you claim are forged, Mr. Gompers?"

The superintendent was flipping rapidly through the loose-leaf records, stopping from time to time to examine a sheet more closely.

"Now, here's one, for example, page seven." He turned several more leaves. "Page twelve is also a forgery." He hesitated over another page. "Page fourteen isn't quite in my usual hand, but I may have written it in a hurry. I wouldn't like to say." He turned more pages before stopping again. "And pages twenty-two and twenty-three also appear to be forgeries. That's all, as far as I can tell without studying them much more closely, but I'm pretty sure I'm right."

"And these pages all have to do with experimental crossings," Mr. Bowen pointed out. "I know this is the field in which you have been particularly interested." He asked his wife, "Have you had occasion to consult these pages since they were written?"

"No, not carefully. I wouldn't know whether changes were made or not."

"What about you, Mr. Gompers?"

"No, I've hardly had occasion to look back, up until now. It is only as the results of these experiments begin to come in that we are interested in checking back on our original data."

"Then the substitute pages could have beeen inserted at any time?"

"Well, the last page that was later forged was written up only a week ago, so it would have had to be sometime after that, presuming all the forgeries were inserted at the same time."

Mrs. Bowen looked appealingly at Ted. "I know you've helped out on a number of police cases, Ted. Have you ever worked on forgeries?"

"Just once," he answered, "and I really didn't have much to do with it. But I do know the name of an expert in the field. He could probably tell you whether these pages are forgeries or not."

"Well, no, I can't see much reason for that," Mr. Bowen decided. "Mr. Gompers says they're forgeries, and I think we should take his word for it. I certainly can't imagine why he would claim they were forged if they weren't."

"On the contrary," said Mr. Gompers, "I think Ted's suggestion is an excellent one. Let's have an expert decide about it. Look at the way in which I have been compromised in the last few days. A bundle was stolen, and I was the only person who even saw it, except for Freddie, and I doubt that he had much idea what was in it. The office safe was entered and records forged, and I am one of the few persons who is constantly in and out of the office. A tank of poison was stolen, and I am the *only* person with access to the strong room. I don't know any way to prove my innocence on the other things, but at least we should be able to clear up this one thing."

"Well, then, I agree," said Mrs. Bowen, "if it is clearly understood that we are doing it at your request. Will you take care of this matter for us then, Ted?"

"Yes, I'll be glad to, the first thing in the morning. But I don't want to keep the ledger overnight. Put it back in the safe."

"Much good that will do," said Mr. Gompers bitterly. "Somebody's been going through this greenhouse as though walls don't mean anything at all to him."

"Is this ledger ordinarily kept locked up?" Ted inquired.

"Yes," Mrs. Bowen replied, "although it's not considered particularly valuable. It's out of the safe much of the day, and I suppose a good many people could have access to it, if they really wanted to. It would be just a question of waiting till Miss Lance was out of the office, since she'd hardly bother to lock it up in such a case."

"What value would this ledger have to anyone else?"

"I can't imagine that it would have any value at all, Ted. Why should anyone care about what crossings we are attempting? It is only the results that are important, and good results are few and far between."

"I doubt that anyone else could even understand most of our entries," Mr. Gompers pointed out. "They are written in a kind of shorthand notation: 'Rows D and E pollinated with the F3 New Light-White Creeper.' Would that mean anything to you?"

"No," Ted agreed.

"And even if the information were of value to anyone, why forge sheets?" Mr. Bowen reasoned. "An interloper could simply copy out the information he wanted, and then beat it, with no one the wiser."

"Yes, and that makes it seem that the purpose of these forgeries was not to provide any particular benefit to the forger, but rather to hurt the Lady Bee Nursery somehow. Just how have you been hurt?"

"I hadn't thought about that," said Mrs. Bowen, pondering. "Do you think you could correct these forged sheets for us, Mr. Gompers?"

He thought about it, and his answer was somewhat doubtful. "I think I could to a certain extent, Mrs. Bowen, but I don't think I could get all of it, and what I did get might be unreliable."

"Would Mr. Thorton be of any help?"

"It's true that he worked with me on most of this stuff, but he knows very little about it, and I am sure his information would be much less reliable than my own."

"Then I suppose we have been hurt somewhat, Ted," Mrs. Bowen said. "Even if we were to develop a perfect rose, and could propagate it by cuttings and budding, still there are reasons why it would be helpful to know where that rose came from. And in cases where we notice something we like, even though it is not quite perfected, we know what the logical next step is. I suppose many of our experiments will have to be repeated, and this whole field is so exasperatingly involved that it isn't even certain the experiments would come out the same the next time."

"Maybe that's why a perfect rose is so valuable," Nelson offered.

"Yes, a perfect rose—by which I mean a commercially acceptable rose—is worth a good many thousands of dollars to us. That is the pot of gold at the end of the rainbow."

As Ted and Nelson got ready for bed, Nelson made a point of opening wide every window in the cottage.

"I thought you were afraid of werewolves," Ted joked.

"Not of werewolves but whatever it was howling in the swamp," he retorted, "but I'm even more afraid of that missing tank of poisonous spray. I want lots and lots of fresh air around me."

"Sure you wouldn't want to go out and scout around a little?"

"You kidding? The police probably are watching this place, and if anything suspicious turned up, they might shoot first and ask questions afterward. Bed sounds like the safest place to spend the night."

"At least if the police are watching, we won't have to worry about a prowler." But Nelson only gave him a scowl.

Nothing happened to disturb their sleep, and they were up early and reasonably bright. They went out to breakfast, and returned at the usual starting time. The search for the stolen tank was just about getting organized, and Mr. Gompers was in charge of it. Upon seeing Ted, he stopped long enough to get the ledger for him from the office.

"I'll have to know some pages which are yours for sure," Ted advised him, "so the professor will have something to compare with."

"The last two written pages are mine, definitely. That should give him enough to go on. Now remember, don't tell him which pages I said were forgeries. Let him find them for himself."

"I will," Ted promised. He had expected to borrow Nelson's car, but Mrs. Bowen offered one of the greenhouse cars instead.

"Fill up the tank at the station in Lutz. We have credit there."

As Ted walked toward the car, he paused to look at the long greenhouses, service buildings, and sprawling fields. There were so many places that something could be hidden. On the other hand, a cylindrical tank was fairly large and not too easily concealed. Maybe they would find it, if it was anywhere around.

At the service station a young man came out to serve him. Ted got out of the car, and saw no harm in asking a few questions.

"Do you know Fritz Glick?"

"Sure do. He's one of our regular customers."

"Kind of a surly fellow?"

"Oh, that's just his way. He's all right when you get to know him. You've met him?"

"Just once, and I thought maybe that was enough. Does he work around here?"

"A few miles down the road. There's a small chemical lab there. I don't know what they do; he never talks much about that. You might not guess it, but he has a degree in chemistry. All he pretends to be interested in are cars and girls."

Then he noticed for the first time that this was a Lady Bee car. "Oh, you're from the nursery. I haven't noticed you around there before."

"No, I'm just one of the part-time errand boys. You're around there a lot?"

"Every day. My name's John Barley, as in barleycorn. Have you met Miss Lance?"

"Yes, I have."

"Well, then you've met my fiancée. We're getting married December thirty-first."

"Congratulations," Ted murmured. Then this John was the driver of the green roadster that picked Miss Lance up from work every day. What about the Chrysler Imperial? If it had been in the garage—John's garage—wasn't it possible that he had dashed out to the greenhouse in it? Maybe Miss Lance had returned to the office, found the bundle on her desk, and quickly telephoned John to come out and pick it up. If he had done so, he would probably have been careful to use a car that could not have been identified as belonging to him. If true, then John and Miss Lance were probably in it together.

Ted drove past the chemical lab, since it was not much out of his way, but it was small, as John said, and there was no indication of what sort of work was being done inside.

He had called ahead for an appointment at the university with Professor Wiggins who remembered Ted slightly from the previous case, and remarked upon it, then gave the ledger a very casual inspection.

"You do have an authenticated specimen of the person's handwriting?"

"Yes, he assures me that the final two pages are his."

"Well, then, I'll get at it directly. My summer schedule is light, and I may have an answer for you by tonight or tomorrow. Any questions, Ted? You seem to have something on your mind."

"It seems to me there are two kinds of forgeries: where you try to imitate someone else's handwriting, and where you try to disguise your own. How difficult would it be to do the second kind?"

Professor Wiggins smilingly shook his head. "It would be very hard, Ted, perhaps just as hard as the other kind. In that case I would strongly recommend that the person print instead, but even then he might give himself away."

Then a student came in with a question, and Ted shook hands with the professor and left.

CHAPTER 9.

THE JAIL IN HOLIDAY

ON the drive home Ted stopped to purchase a copy of the *Town Crier*. The picture of Mrs. Bowen had turned out well, and he thought she would be pleased with the story, too. Mention was also made of Mrs. King's Blue Lady, and Ted wondered what Mrs. Bowen would have to say about that.

He had already gone a little out of his way, and upon consulting a map he found that he could return to Lady Bee's another way, through the village of Holiday. He thought it might be interesting to see the place where Mr. Bowen had spent his weekend.

Holiday had a post office, a drug store, a service station and a grocery, and not very much else. He stopped at the drug store for a soda and got to talking to the owner.

"Where do you keep your prisoners?" he asked. "I didn't notice any jail."

"Oh, we've never needed a jail in Holiday."

"But suppose you do?"

"Then we send them over to Fulton Roads, the county seat. They've got all the facilities there."

This was certainly not what Mr. Bowen had said, but Ted kept his voice casual.

"You didn't run into any trouble over the weekend?"

"No, nothing that I know of, and believe me I'd know about it if there was anything."

Ted stepped outside and wandered around for a while. He couldn't see any place where Mr. Bowen might have dug up a wild rose, but that didn't prove this part of the story was necessarily untrue. It need not have happened in the middle of the village, and there were woods and wild places beyond.

A little past the outskirts Ted noticed a greenhouse. Could this be the reason for Mr. Bowen's interest in Holiday, if indeed he had really spent the weekend there? What did the greenhouse have to offer?

Returning to the car, Ted drove slowly past. It was a much smaller operation than Lady Bee's. It had only one greenhouse complex, and even this was smaller than any of the Lady Bee complexes. Nor did it have the total acreage, although there seemed to be room for expansion. Only a few workers were visible in the fields. The greenhouse itself was by no means dilapidated; rather, it seemed to be fairly new.

Ted arrived back at close to lunch time, and he and Nelson went out to eat.

"Nothing doing on the search?"

"Not a thing, Ted. We looked just about every conceivable place, but no tank. About the only place it could be hidden on the estate is buried somewhere."

"Inside or out?"

"That's so, it could be in one of the greenhouses. Some of those floor beds go right into the ground, and you'd dig someplace where digging wouldn't seem at all suspicious. Well, I don't know why anybody would steal it to bury it."

"Unless they wanted to unbury it sometime in the future."

"True enough," said Nelson.

"You didn't find anything else, either?"

"How do you mean that, Ted?"

"Well, there's a big bundle of clippings missing, too, you know."

"I thought we had it figured out that it went out the front door to a car."

"That's so, if the car was the Chrysler Imperial. No other car was seen around."

"And that's enough. I'm betting on Fritz Glick. That bundle couldn't have disappeared into thin air."

Ted laughed. "I've been thinking about it, and I believe that's exactly what might have happened. We've been looking for a big bundle. What if the bundle was opened up and taken apart? A few clippings could be disposed of around here, a few around there—you always see things like that around a greenhouse. Once the wrappings and labels are disposed of, there's no bundle left even to disappear."

"You're forgetting that bolted door behind the office, Ted."

"No, I was thinking of perhaps someone coming into the office, opening the bundle, hiding the wrappings under his shirt, and taking out a few clippings at a time. It probably would have taken a number of trips, but with so many people going past, he might hardly be noticed. A car might be observed, but no one was keeping track of who went into and out of the office."

"What if Miss Lance came back between his trips?"

"Pretend you don't know anything about it."

Nelson shrugged and changed the subject. "How'd you make out on the forgeries, Ted?"

"I left the ledger with Professor Wiggins, and I'll call him tonight or tomorrow. But I'm pretty sure how it will come out. He'll find that the same pages are forged that Mr. Gompers claimed. I don't think Mr. Gompers would have put himself on the spot like that, unless he was sure of himself."

"Any chance Mr. Gompers could have deliberately made those pages look like forgeries?"

"I doubt it. To get away with it, Mr. Gompers would have to be a smarter man than the professor, and I don't think he is."

"I didn't know they taught forgery at college. What is Wiggins a professor of?"

"Archaeology, and I think he's worked on some ancient scripts."

Ted went on to tell Nelson about his discovery at Holiday.

"Mr. Bowen obviously spent the weekend away from home and doesn't want his wife to know where. All right, is that any of our business, Ted?"

"You're perfectly right about that, as long as it doesn't have anything to do with all these other things going on."

"Just what *has* been going on, Ted? A lot of strange doings, but they don't seem to add up to any serious crime—not until the thief uses that poisonous spray. A wolf or a man that can walk through doors is pretty scary, but I can't see the profit to anyone."

Then Ted remembered his conversation with John Barley, and told Nelson about it.

"Say, Ted, this chemical lab where Fritz Glick works—do you suppose it could have anything to do with poisonous sprays?"

"I don't know. I couldn't find out anything. Anyway, I don't see what that would have to do with the theft here."

"But he does work near here, and he said his car was in a garage Friday afternoon, which probably means John's garage. It seems like a simple thing, Ted. Let's ask John if the car was there."

"You want to give it away like that?"

"Sure. What have we got to lose? Either he tells us or he doesn't."

"But what he tells us might be the truth or a lie, and meanwhile we've got him alerted." But in the end Ted gave in. Fundamentally, he supposed, he believed in John Barley's innocence, and it might be helpful to see what explanation he had to offer.

"Let's do it right now," Nelson urged.

So they left the counter and drove to the service station. John was on duty, and recognized Ted this time, though he had not been on duty when Nelson had come in. They got out of the car, and waited till John was free.

"John," said Ted, having introduced Nelson, "would you mind telling us if Fritz Glick's car was in your station Friday afternoon?"

John hesitated, looking from one to the other. It seemed to be a difficult question for him to answer, as though it might lead him into uncharted and treacherous shoal waters.

"Did he say it was here?"

"He said it was in the garage, so we supposed it was here."

"All right, then, it was here."

"Did Fritz drive it at all on Friday afternoon?"

"Not till he was through with working. He couldn't have taken it before then."

"Well, did anybody drive it?"

This was the point that John had evidently anticipated and feared.

"All right, I drove it."

"To the greenhouse?"

"Yes. You must have guessed that already. Now there wasn't anything wrong about that. I wanted to take it out on the road for a little trial, and the greenhouse is just a short drive. My girl was there, and I could show her the car; you don't need much of an excuse to see the person you're engaged to. However, she wasn't in the office and I couldn't stand around waiting, so I drove right off."

"Did you see a large bundle on her desk?"

"I know about the missing bundle, because Clarice told me about it. If it was on her desk I should have seen it, but you know how it is when you have something else on your mind. Sometimes you wouldn't notice an elephant crossing your path. I didn't see it, and I don't think it was there, but I couldn't answer to it."

"Why didn't you tell Mrs. Bowen about this before?"

"Clarice thought I should, but since I hadn't seen anything, I didn't see how that would do any good, except that you could stop looking for the red car. I suppose the main reason was that I didn't want to get Fritz Glick involved. He's got the kind of mouth that gets people down on him, but I knew he couldn't have had anything to do with the missing bundle. However, something else has come up, and I had just about made up my mind to tell.

"Last night I got an anonymous telephone call. As far as I recall, the voice said exactly these words: 'You'd better tell your girl friend to keep her nose out of things if you want her to stay healthy.' Then he hung up."

"A man?"

"Undoubtedly."

"You don't have any idea what he referred to?"

"It must have something to do with some of these odd things going on out at the greenhouse that she's been telling me about. But I don't know of anything she could be doing, outside of her regular duties."

"Have you done anything about that anonymous call?"

John looked perplexed. "No, I can't make up my mind what I ought to do. I hate to get Clarice upset or worried. But if it is serious, I ought to put her on her guard. What can you do in a case like that?"

"What about the police?" asked Nelson.

"Well, that would amount to the same thing as telling her first, because they would go right to her about it. And what could the police do? They can't trace the call anymore, and they can't put a twenty-four-hour guard on every person who received a threat, or else they'd never get anything else done. What would you do?"

But neither Ted nor Nelson had any helpful advice to offer.

"What do you expect to do?" Ted questioned.

"Oh, I don't think I want to tell Clarice, at least unless the thing gets more serious. I'll just keep on picking her up at work, and make sure she doesn't go out alone evenings. And keep my eyes open.

Maybe something will break somewhere. That's some yarn about the werewolf, isn't it?"

"Do you know Tammi?" Nelson inquired.

"Tammi? Is she the one who's spreading that story?" John's face fell. "Then I might as well wise you up. You can't believe a word she says."

"How well do you know her?"

"We were in high school together. She was in the ninth grade when I was in the twelfth."

"Then Tammi is still in high school?" asked Ted.

"Yes. Is she passing herself off as a college girl?" John shrugged, as though that was all you could expect.

Ted and Nelson were disappointed, too, and discussed the matter further on their way back.

"There goes the whole werewolf bit," Nelson declared bitterly. "It never was anything but a figment of her imagination—if that."

"What about the howling we heard in the swamp?"

Nelson brightened. "Well, yes, there is still something left, isn't there? And the salami, and whoever it is entering the safe and the strong room, plus the stolen bundle. There's still a prowler around."

As they drove into the parking lot they were fortunate enough to see Tammi across the way. Nelson leaped out.

"Come on, Ted, I'm going to have it out with her right now."

She turned and waited for them when she saw them coming. Nelson's first words were: "Tammi, why did you lie to us about being in college?"

She opened her eyes wide. "Who's been telling you things about me?"

"Well, you aren't in college, are you?"

"No."

"Then why did you say you were?"

"Because you're college boys, and I thought you'd be more interested in a college girl than a high-school girl. I don't see why it's a lie when you try to make yourself more interesting, any more than it's a lie to put on lipstick."

"But you made up the whole story about the werewolf, too, didn't you?"

"No, Nelson, I didn't, really. I did see a large animal in the moonlight that looked like a wolf, and I did see a man, and I didn't see the two of them together, so the wolf could have changed into a man, couldn't it? I don't suppose it was really a werewolf, because they say there aren't such things, but how can they tell for sure? There's no way to prove there aren't any, somewhere."

"Did the man disappear?"

"Yes."

"Right through the wall?"

"Well, he walked right up to the wall, and then suddenly he was gone. That meant he must have gone through the wall, doesn't it?"

"But you didn't see him inside?"

"Not really. I just knew he must be in there."

And that, apparently, was as straight a story as they were going to get about the werewolf—from Tammi.

CHAPTER 10.

GOVERNOR HOPE

MRS. Bowen read Ted's story with much interest, and thanked him for it. She had nothing to say about Blue Lady until Ted remarked upon it.

"Yes, that's very interesting, Ted. I'll be most pleased to see it at the show. Naturally I knew there would be other lavender roses, but I still have a great deal of faith in Governor Hope. Would you like to see it?"

They agreed eagerly.

Their eyes bugged out when they saw it. This wasn't Governor Hope. It was Blue Lady. But whatever it was, they looked remarkably alike. Was there some subtle difference between the two that their inexpert eyes could not detect?

"That's a very nice flower, Mrs. Bowen," said Ted, appreciatively, for that it was, but his voice undoubtedly conveyed some sense of doubt which Mrs. Bowen was quick to pick up.

"You mustn't let unusual things disturb you just because they seem strange. You have to bring to them the same objective standards you would bring to conventional things."

"Oh, it doesn't bother us, Mrs. Bowen. We've already seen Blue Lady, so we're used to it."

"Then you think Blue Lady is a better rose than Governor Hope?" she asked quickly.

"Not better but equal."

"*Exactly* equal," said Nelson with unintended emphasis.

Then Mrs. Bowen understood. "I see." She studied them closely, and they in turn studied Governor Hope. "Now that you've observed them more carefully, can you notice anything different?"

They wanted to so badly that they almost imagined they did. But as far as they could tell these were precisely the same rose.

"I hardly know what to do." A slight tremor in her voice betrayed her concern. "If this rose is so close to the other that the public could confuse them, I might be hurting myself by exhibiting it. However, I did have hopes of patenting it, and that would mean a great deal to me."

"Look, Mrs. Bowen," said Ted firmly, "we're not experts by any means, and we could be wrong. But it might be a good thing for you if you would look into this thing yourself. Could you come up to Forestdale?"

"If that is the only way—"

"I've got a picture of Blue Lady, Mrs. Bowen," Nelson broke in. "A colored picture. Would that help you?"

"It might, Nelson. Where is your picture?"

"At a photography shop in Forestdale. Of course I haven't seen it yet, but if it wasn't good enough, I could go over to Mrs. King's and take another one. I forgot, I'm working here, and I'm supposed to be repairing windows. Ted, what are you doing this afternoon?"

Mrs. Bowen smiled. "I don't think I want you up on those roofs in this mid-day heat anyway, Nelson. If you want to run up to Forestdale this afternoon, it's perfectly all right with me. You can go in the pick-up, and make some deliveries for me and purchase some things I need."

"What about you, Ted?"

"I'll come along. There are a few things I'd like to do at the newspaper office."

"Do you know where Mrs. King got her Blue Lady?" asked Mrs. Bowen.

"She said that her sister bought it on the West Coast. We could stop in and ask her more about it."

"I would appreciate it if you would. I try my best to stay up to date on roses, but this might be something I should have heard about but didn't."

When they were out on the road in the pick-up, Nelson said, "Don't you feel that we're getting our teeth into things at last, Ted? Up till now there wasn't anything stolen that amounted to beans, but now we're on the track of something valuable."

"I think you're right about that. I felt right along we were missing the most important thing of all."

"Here's what I don't get, Ted. If patents are so important, why didn't Mrs. B. run right down to the patent office with her new rose?"

"Remember she develops hundreds of new roses every year. She can't patent them all. She only does that with the ones she thinks are distinctive and worthwhile. And she didn't know until the past few weeks that Governor Hope was going to be one of those special ones."

They made their deliveries along the way. In Forestdale Ted stopped in at the newspaper office, while Nelson made the purchases for Mrs. Bowen. Although they had planned to stop in to see Mrs. King, Ted wondered if the telephone might not be just as good. It would save time, and it was less likely that Mrs. King would prolong the conversation and ask questions that they would rather not answer at this point. He dialed her number.

"Mrs. King? This is Ted Wilford."

"Yes, Ted, glad to hear from you. I was just reading your story in the morning *Town Crier,* although I've already read it half a dozen times."

"I'm very glad you liked it, Mrs. King. I was talking with Mrs. Bowen this morning and she was curious about where your sister purchased Blue Lady."

"I don't think she ever told me. Perhaps she doesn't quite remember. But I'll call her again if you want me to."

"If you wouldn't mind giving me her telephone number, perhaps I could call her myself. I'm just leaving the *Town Crier* office, and you might not be able to reach me."

"Well, it's a toll call. She lives in Winter's Ledge."

"Why, that's not too much out of our way. We're heading back for Lutz in a little while. Perhaps we can stop on the way, and if she isn't home I can call her later."

"That would be perfectly satisfactory, Ted. I'm sure she would be pleased. I always send her the *Town Crier,* so she knows you by name already. Her name is Mrs. Tolman. Main Street."

"Thank you, Mrs. King. This is very kind of you. Good luck with Blue Lady."

When Nelson stopped at the *Town Crier* for Ted, he had his photographs with him. They examined the picture of Blue Lady, and as far as their untrained eyes could tell, it was no different from Governor Hope. Mr. Dobson and Miss Monroe had heard the story of the similar roses, and though they admired the picture, they had no basis for comparison.

They were lucky enough to find Mrs. Tolman in. She did recognize Ted's name, was introduced to Nelson, and invited them in, but when they had stated the reason for their call, she shook her head slowly.

"I'm afraid I can't help you there at all."

"You mean you don't know where you got the rose?" Ted questioned.

"Oh, yes, I know exactly where I got it."

"In California?"

"No, not at all." She smiled. "Let me explain. My husband and I made a trip out to California. It was rather a hurried trip, and I didn't have time for as much shopping as I would have liked. My sister is a person of excellent taste and strong opinions, so you can imagine that she is difficult to buy for. I knew she would be disappointed if I didn't bring her back something, but I just hadn't been able to find anything satisfactory, and here I was back home.

"I explained my problem to my neighbor, Mr. Player, who already knew that she liked roses. He had just bought several new rose bushes himself, and offered to let me have one. I jumped at the chance. I had little expectation that it would amount to much, but at least it would show my sister that my heart was in the right place. And I'm afraid I did let her think it came from California, when actually it came from next door."

"Do you know where your neighbor purchased it?"

"He didn't say. I felt that he had probably picked up some culls at a sale. He refused to accept payment, which made me think it was probably very cheap. You can imagine my pleasure and surprise when my sister called me to rave over it."

"Can't we ask your neighbor about it?"

She shook her head again. "He's moved away. I have no idea where, although I know it must be a good distance."

"One thing we're ahead, Ted," Nelson said as they drove away. "If that Blue Lady really had come from California, it wasn't likely it had anything to do with Mrs. B. It could hardly have spread that far in such a short time, and if it had, it would have been a remarkable coincidence that Mrs. Tolman had just happened to bring it back. But if it came from this area somewhere, then there's a much better chance that it was stolen from Lady Bee's."

"It was a little odd that we should have been the ones to discover it, but it only happened because we were particularly interested in lavender roses. Otherwise we wouldn't have paid any special attention to it."

"If it is the same rose, Ted. I'm hoping for Mrs. B.'s sake that it isn't."

They were soon able to put the matter to an expert test. On arriving at the greenhouse, they went immediately to the office and showed the photograph to Mrs. Bowen. She studied it for several minutes, and seemed obviously surprised. Apparently she had convinced herself that Ted and Nelson were mistaken, and this new evidence was both disturbing and disagreeable.

"It does look just like Governor Hope," she admitted at last, "but sometimes the color on these photographs is not exact. Was this taken by daylight or flash?"

"In the evening with supplemental flash."

"That might make it even more difficult. Do you think this is an accurate rendition of the color?"

"I think it is. What about you, Ted?"

"Don't ask me. You've got a much better eye for these things than I have."

"Did you happen to notice the thorns?" she inquired. "This picture hardly shows them at all."

"Why, no, I didn't. I was only interested in the picture. And you didn't either, did you, Ted? You were too busy gabbing."

"Well. . . ." She seemed to be arriving at a decision which was unpleasant to her. "I couldn't exhibit Governor Hope under these conditions. To have two such roses in the same show would stir up too many questions. I'm terribly sorry. The governor is going to attend himself, and he will be expecting to see the rose named after him, but I don't see any other way out of it."

"Mrs. King won't be attempting to patent it, will she?"

"I should hardly think so, since she has no idea where it came from. But the source of that rose may be seeking a patent on it, if the person involved has any idea of its value."

"He may not, if it was sold as a cull," Ted reminded her.

"Well, that is another possible angle. No, I'll have to consider this matter fully, and perhaps take it up with my patent attorney. You say this was the first year Mrs. King's plant bloomed?"

"That's what she told us."

"Well, it was the first year for mine, too, on a scale sufficient to judge it, so there might be something in that. Evidently Mrs. King has had her plant since last year, but if it was a cutting that was stolen, it might have been as much as a year or two before that!"

This seemed to indicate to Ted and Nelson that a prowler had been hanging around for a considerable time.

CHAPTER 11.

THE PROWLER WALKS AGAIN

AND now for the windows," Nelson decided.

"Don't tell me you're going to start repairing windows this late in the afternoon?"

"Why not? The work's there to be done, and I might as well do what I can. Wait'll I slip on some coveralls."

"Want me to help?" Ted offered.

"No, why should you? You're wearing your good suit, and furthermore I haven't time to teach you how to put in greenhouse windows. Good enough?"

"Good enough," Ted agreed. "I'll remember to wear my good suit when there's work to be done. What should I do?"

"I'll let you help move the ladders, if you want to be useful."

So Nelson was soon busy scrambling up the slanting greenhouse roofs and enjoying himself immensely. At first he kept up a running line of chatter, as Ted stood below, but talking so loud soon became tiresome, and he had to keep his mind on his work. Scrambling over the peak of one roof and down the opposite slope, he disappeared from Ted's sight.

The next thing Ted knew a pebble fell beside him. He looked up and saw Nelson's head just sticking over the peak once more, finger to his lips in caution. Having secured Ted's attention, Nelson pointed dramatically in the direction of the strong room. Ted nodded, and then eased his way to the corner of the greenhouse and looked carefully around it. Mr. Gompers was at the door of the strong room— and he had set a large tank on the ground beside him as he opened the locks. He opened the door, picked up the tank, and went inside. A moment later he came out again, empty-handed, fastened the door, looked around, and started off in the opposite direction.

Nelson was soon on the ground again and at Ted's side. "Well, what do you make of that, Ted?"

"Obviously, he is up to no good."

"They were fumigating today, but not this house, and they finished earlier. I noticed them carrying the tanks back when we drove in. It looks to me as though he carried this tank in from his car. Furthermore he was looking around as though he was being careful not to be seen. If anybody ever looked guilty, he did."

"I don't know why he'd want to put back a tank he had stolen, and if he did, he should have waited till dark."

"Till the burglar alarm goes on? That might be too late for him. And he didn't run too much of a risk. It was only a short way from his car to the room, and everybody's over at the conservatory this time of evening."

Suddenly Mr. Gompers rounded the corner of the greenhouse, almost bumping into them. Evidently he had changed his mind and decided to come back this way. He looked at them for a moment, and then at the ladders reaching up to the roof and over the peak.

"Were you up there working just now?"

"Yes, I was," Nelson admitted.

"It's after quitting time. It's better not to hang around after regular hours. It leads to all kinds of complications." He seemed to ponder for a moment. "Were you up there when I went into the strong room?"

"Yes," said Nelson.

"Then no doubt you saw me carrying in a tank of spray. You must have wondered if it was the tank that was stolen and we spent so much time looking for this morning."

"We wondered," Ted admitted.

"Then let me put you straight on that. It is the same tank, the stolen tank. I found it in the trunk of my car. Doubtless it has been there ever since it was stolen, for I haven't been in my trunk for several days."

"Was any of the poison missing?"

"No, the tank is exactly as full as at the time it was first stolen. It has a gauge to tell."

"Wasn't the trunk of your car locked?" Nelson questioned.

"It locks automatically. But what are locks to a fellow like this? If he can get into the strong room, possibly at a time when the burglar alarm was set, a simple car lock isn't going to stop him."

"Are you going to report it to Mrs. Bowen?" asked Ted.

"Of course I shall. Now. Previously I hadn't quite made up my mind. I discovered it when I was about to leave for supper, and decided it would be best to put it back during conservatory when no one was around. But I suppose I would have told Mrs. B. Surely she couldn't believe I stole the tank just so I could put it back again. What would be the point of it?"

"Maybe you weren't able to dispose of it," Nelson said.

"That's hardly the case. I've driven my car home every evening, as I was about to do again. I would have had plenty of opportunity to dispose of it if I had stolen it. And even if I didn't steal it, there would have been less risk to me if I were to get rid of it somewhere else rather than to get caught with it in my possession."

"Why didn't you?" asked Ted.

"I could say I was honest and didn't like to take her property. But an even more compelling reason is that I imagine that was exactly what the fellow wants me to do—the one who put the tank in my car."

"What do you think his idea was?" Nelson inquired.

"I think that's becoming increasingly obvious every day. Someone wants me out of here. I don't know why. I can't see how I represent a threat to anyone. But it could be one of the workers under me, perhaps someone with a grudge against me, or else someone who hopes to get my job. Well, I'll report it to Mrs. Bowen. We still don't know how the tank was stolen, but at least there need be no mystery about how it got back."

As he stalked off, Nelson remarked, "Something else that doesn't make much sense, unless we accept his explanation for it."

"There's another possible explanation. Somebody stole the tank because he did have a use for it, and hid it in Mr. Gompers' car, either because that was the most convenient place, or maybe it was an emergency and that was the only place he could find. He intended to get it out of there later, but never found the chance."

"We're sure that Mr. Gompers isn't the man who went into the safe, aren't we?"

"I don't see how he could be. He could have normally gone in any time he wanted to and no questions asked."

"But Miss Lance was usually in the office."

"Usually, but not always. All he had to do was wait for his chance. I imagine she sometimes went out and left the safe unlocked. And what did he want in there anyway? Apparently just to substitute those forged pages. I think I'll call the professor and see what he's found out."

The call was put through from a booth adjoining the greenhouse, and Professor Wiggins was soon on the wire.

"Yes, Ted, I can give you a preliminary report. The forged pages are numbered seven, twelve, fourteen, twenty-two, and twenty-three."

Ted had written down the numbers Mr. Gompers had previously given, and was consulting the list now. The numbers were exactly the same.

"That checks out with what we were told. Did anything else show up?"

"No, except for those pages, everything seems to be in order. I'll have a report ready by noon tomorrow, and you can pick up the ledger anytime after that."

"Well, Mr. Gompers called the turn all right on the forgeries," Ted relayed to Nelson after hanging up. "I knew he must be in the clear when he called Mrs. B's attention to it."

"He didn't exactly call attention to it, Ted. Mrs. B. may have put him on the spot when she questioned some of his data, and he had to say something."

"But if he'd made the forgeries, don't you think he'd have had a good explanation ready? Add to that how upset he was, and I think we can rule out the idea he had anything to do with those forged pages."

"Then that also rules out the chance that he's the greenhouse prowler, too."

"Oh, I gave up on that idea long ago. He's the one person who can come and go wherever he pleases on this property. He'd have no reason to sneak around after dark."

"I don't see that anyone else would, either, Ted. If the theft of Governor Hope was the big crime, that happened long ago. Presumably the thief would beat it out of here after that."

"Unless he was after something bigger."

"Only there isn't anything bigger than Governor Hope."

"True enough, unless we're speaking of the whole operation. Are you finished?"

"I guess so. Mr. Gompers told me to quit, and he's my working boss. I don't think it would hurt to leave the ladders in place. Let's go to the cottage and wash up, then go out for a bite to eat, come back and enjoy the conservatory for a while, and get to bed early. I've got lots and lots of work to do tomorrow. What's your schedule?"

"I've always got work waiting for me at the office, if I'm not needed here."

The evening passed, and they were ready for bed at an unusually early hour, with twilight still hanging in the sky.

"Do we sleep with the windows open or closed?" Ted demanded.

"Closed. As long as the poison spray has been returned, my mind is back on that howling in the swamp."

Ted fell asleep quickly, as though he had a clear conscience, "or no conscience," as Nelson sometimes expressed it. But Nelson was more restive, and Ted was half-aroused several times by his tossing in the lower bunk. At least twice Ted heard him get up to go to the window and look out. The moon had grown to a respectable size, and in the earlier half of the night, at least, cast its inquisitive light on the several greenhouses and the many acres of plants that stretched from the road to the fir trees.

The next thing Ted knew, he was being aroused in earnest as Nelson shook his shoulder vigorously.

"Come on, Ted, wake up. He's back!"

"Who's back?" Ted demanded, still trying to figure out where he was.

"The wolf, or dog, or whatever he is. I just saw him leaping over the hedge."

At last Ted got the message, and followed Nelson to the window. "Where is he?"

"He ran across the field, and then leaped the hedge and disappeared."

"The same place Tammi saw him disappear?"

"No, I don't think so. What difference does it make? Come on, let's go out there and get hold of this thing."

"I thought you were afraid of wolves."

"I'm afraid of their leaping through the window when I'm asleep. I'm not afraid of them when I'm awake."

"Especially when it may be only a dog."

"That may be, but I never saw a dog leap a hedge like that."

Ted might have added Nelson had never seen a wolf leap like that, either, but Nelson was busy getting on some clothes, and Ted followed his example.

"Remember we don't have any weapons," he said.

"We'll find something, a club, maybe."

In the cottage's small vestibule stood a number of garden tools. Nelson selected a shovel for himself, and handed Ted a rake. These might not be the most appropriate weapons, but they were the best available.

As they stepped outside, the moonlight added to their feeling of unreality, as though they themselves were actors in some fantasy. Everything was country-still, and they were not aware of any wind, though the tips of the firs swayed and bowed in tribute to some unseen breeze. The stars shone brightly, except where they were obscured in a circle around the first-quarter moon.

Ted was fully awake at last. "I don't like this moonlight. Anybody could see us coming all across the field, and the shrubs are too small to hide behind."

"Then let's keep behind the hedge, in the shadow of the firs," Nelson suggested. "We can get all the way to the other side, and turn down the back path toward the greenhouses."

This was acceptable to Ted, and they crept along, bending their heads low, but glancing occasionally across the intervening hedge.

"Are we looking for a dog or a wolf or a man?" Ted inquired, wondering about their improvised weapons.

"Maybe a dog and a man. I'm not afraid of a dog, if it's owned by a man. I'm beginning to think this is a partnership. Tammi *almost* saw them together, and I believe they're still together. After all, this is a pretty tough world for a dog to make a living in, all by himself."

"All right, then, we're looking for a man who may be protected by a large dog. Just don't do anything reckless."

"Ted, look!"

Nelson's grip cut into Ted's arm as he drew him firmly down beside him. They knelt on the ground, their eyes barely clearing the hedge. Ted looked in the direction Nelson indicated, toward that same little hedge where Tammi had claimed to have seen the wolf disappear. There was no sign of the wolf-dog, but a man had pushed out from between the hedges and was heading toward the nearest greenhouse.

"Want to get closer, Ted?"

"Not on your life. That dog's probably still behind the hedge, protecting his rear."

"Want to look?"

"What for? It's what the man's doing that's important. You think we're going to see him walk right through the wall, the way Tammi claimed?"

"I don't know. There certainly aren't any doors, where he's heading, and I've a hunch he's afraid to go around the end of the greenhouses, where he might be visible from the road. If that's true, he won't be going near the strong room."

Ted reflected. "What's in this greenhouse?"

"Just seedlings and small plants from what I've seen. The next building contains the Fun House and the orchid room. And the third building is the one just behind the office, the one where they do most of their indoor experimenting, and where Mrs. B. has her Governor Hope."

"It's most likely to be the last building he's interested in, and he cuts through the first two to avoid getting out in the open."

"Then he isn't going to get through tonight, Ted. The next building is the one that was fumigated today. One whiff of that and he'll change his mind in a hurry."

But the intruder had at least one surprise for them. He did not go directly toward the building and disappear through the wall, which would have been amazing even though expected. Instead, he seemed to have noticed the ladders Nelson had left in place, and was heading toward them. At the foot of the ladder, he tested it once to make sure it was solid, then slowly climbed. On the roof he transferred to the glazing ladder and slowly made his way to the peak. For a moment he stood silhouetted against the night sky, and then he disappeared down the other side.

"Now what?" asked Ted.

"There's no place to go. There's another ladder running down to the next furrow, and that's the end. He's stuck in that little valley, unless he wants to take a chance and walk on glass. I wouldn't recommend it."

"There must be a place to go. He seems to know exactly what he's doing. Aren't there roof ventilators, all the way along there? I'm betting he'll open one of those and drop down inside the greenhouse."

"Say, you could be right, Ted. It wouldn't be too much of a drop, if you knew for sure what was below, and it certainly looks like he knows. But he won't be able to get out the same way."

"I don't think getting out represents much of a problem. The side ventilators seem to open quite easily from the inside, and I don't suppose they are all connected to the burglar alarm."

"One thing's for sure—he won't come out a door. They must be connected to the alarm, or there wouldn't be much sense in having it."

They sat there, minute after minute, vaguely dissatisfied. Nothing was happening that they could see, and they were doing nothing about catching this trespasser. Yet they did not care to do anything to alarm the dog, who might not be dangerous, but surely could bark or howl.

Convinced as they were that the second fumigated greenhouse would stop the intruder and lead him to change his plans, and that he would come back this way to pick up his dog, this seemed the best possible place. With luck, he would pass close enough so they could get a look at his face. Nothing they had seen so far was of much use for identification, except that he seemed a spry young man of moderate build.

Time dragged on. All they could do was sit tight and hope. The minutes passed . . . ten, fifteen . . . then the burglar alarm clanged violently.

CHAPTER 12.

SWAMPLAND

ALL hope of catching the intruder at his work had now vanished. Undoubtedly he would cut and run, but which way he would run was the problem. There was no assurance now that he would come back this way to pick up his dog.

They cast an apprehensive look toward the hedge behind which they thought the dog was hiding. If so, he was still there, crouched down, waiting.

"Which way do we go, Ted?"

"I suppose he'll try to run out one of the greenhouse doors, at one end or the other."

"More likely this end, Ted. That's nearer the place where he went in."

"It's also on the moonlit side, but maybe he doesn't have much choice."

"Unless he wants to stay hidden inside the greenhouse, and take his chances on being found. He must have tripped some kind of alarm inside the greenhouse. Surely he would know better than to try one of the doors."

"Well, let's try this end, then," Ted agreed. "It looks as though the Bowen house is lit up. They may catch him if he comes out the other side."

They pushed through the hedge, and with occasional apprehensive glances over toward the dog's supposed hiding place, they walked rapidly to the moonlit end of the greenhouses, beyond the strong room. As far as they could tell, nothing had been disturbed at this end: no doors were open; there were no signs of a forced entry or exit. The burglar alarm suddenly stopped ringing.

"I think we should have tried the other ends," Nelson decided swiftly, but it was too late for that now. The intruder had more than likely made his escape. In any event, someone was coming toward them from the house.

"Freeze, Ted," Nelson commanded. "We don't want them thinking we're the prowler, and taking a shot at us."

This seemed excellent advice to Ted, and he and Nelson stood stock still in the moonlight as Mr. and Mrs. Bowen came up.

The owners recognized them promptly, and continued to approach.

"Any sign of him?" Mr. Bowen called.

"Not now," Nelson returned. "We saw him go in through a roof ventilator, but we didn't see him come out anywhere. I don't think he could have come back that way."

"We thought at first you were the ones, and that's why we came this way. Well, I suppose he's gone by now. It would be a simple matter to unbolt one of the doors and leave, and wouldn't make any difference as long as the burglar alarm was ringing anyway."

"Let's walk all the way around the greenhouses and see if there's any sign," Mrs. Bowen suggested. "The police will be here soon. I called them before we came out."

"We think there may be a big dog, behind that hedge," Ted indicated, but no one wanted to tackle a large, frightened dog, and anyway the man seemed more important. Nor did there seem to be any point in dividing into two groups, convinced as they were that the man had already gotten away.

Mr. Bowen tested each greenhouse door on this end, and nothing gave. They then walked down the long path between two of the houses to the other end. It was immediately apparent to them that some of their surmises had been incorrect, for a door of the middle house was swinging wide open.

"The fumigated house!" Mrs. Bowen exclaimed. "Oh, great heavens!"

"He probably got out in time," Mr. Bowen assured her, hurrying toward the door.

The boys with him got just a whiff of the repellent spray before he closed the door.

"He may be in there yet," Mrs. Bowen cried.

"He couldn't be. He didn't collapse near the door. He must have gotten in some other way, realized that he was in trouble, and came to the door, unbolted it, and ran out. Luckily this isn't the door that is locked from outside. Opening the door was what tripped the alarm."

"How much of it could he take?" asked Ted.

Mr. Bowen shook his head. "It is partly settled already, but five minutes of it might get him into trouble. Even if he got out he may collapse outside somewhere. We'll have to look for him. Thank goodness, there's the police car."

The car pulled into the yard, and two officers jumped out and ran to them. Explanations were quickly made. The officer in charge studied the situation, and agreed with Mr. Bowen that it was nearly impossible the intruder was still inside the fumigated house. However, Mrs. Bowen remained dissatisfied.

"He might have opened the door, then become frightened or confused when the alarm rang, and gone back in."

"What can you do about it?" the officer inquired.

"We can get a man with a mask on to go in and look," Mr. Bowen explained. "I'd do it myself, but our strong room where the equipment is kept is locked, and the man with the key isn't here."

Although the officers might have broken into the strong room, it would take them a while, and it seemed that it would be just as quick to call Mr. Gompers who lived close by, and have him come over.

"It will be too late for that man if he's still in there," Nelson argued in a whisper to Ted. "However, I'm sure he got out."

Mrs. Bowen hurried to the house to make the call. The officers' minds were traveling in another direction.

"There's little doubt he got out, but he may still be around somewhere. We'll have to look to see if he's lying somewhere on the ground. You don't have any idea which direction he might have taken?"

Ted and Nelson shook their heads. They had seen the dog leaping the far hedge, they explained, but that was no proof the intruder had tried to escape in that direction.

"It would appear to me," the officer deduced, "that he came in a car, parked it down the road somewhere, and circled around the back to get in here. If he's in his car now, that may be very bad. If he faints at the wheel, it could be fatal, for him or someone else. If he faints on the ground that might not be so bad; the fresh air would help revive him, if he didn't have too big a whiff."

The police decided to search the nearby roads. Mr. Gompers would soon be there to look inside the greenhouse, and meanwhile the others could search outside. Nelson got two strong flashlights from his car and gave one to Ted. Mr. and Mrs. Bowen would look toward the road, while the boys searched the back area. It was true that they hadn't seen the intruder retreat that way, but he could have done so after they had left their posts and gone to the wrong ends of the greenhouses.

"Let's see about that dog first," said Nelson grimly, and this time Ted was willing. Both boys were still carrying the weapons they had brought from the cottage, and upon reaching the small hedge they poked into it gingerly. There was no sight or sound of the dog, and they pushed through the hedge completely.

The dog was not there. Whether or not he ever had been, there was no way to tell. The dirt had been trampled, but when it had happened could not be ascertained, nor could they find any indication of paw prints in the dust.

"I'm sure he *was* here, though," Nelson insisted. "I'll bet he's one of those real smart dogs who knew enough to wait till the coast was clear, and then lit out."

"Or the man may have come back for him," Ted said.

This was the eastern edge of the Lady Bee estate, and since there was no sign of the man on the estate, they searched beyond. Here was unused land, of grass, low shrubs, and brush. A search by only two people, in the darkness, was very nearly useless.

"We might not even see him, unless we stumbled over him," Nelson observed.

"No, except that there is a dog, and the dog didn't get any of the poisonous fumes, I'm pretty sure. The dog would probably stick close to his master."

"If the dog and the man really are a pair," Nelson pointed out. "We don't have any proof of that."

"But the dog and the man have been seen almost together," Ted reasoned.

Nelson agreed because it seemed that that was probably their only hope of finding the man anyway. He had to be still with the dog. If he was out here alone lying on the ground, they would hardly find him before daylight, and by that time he might have revived and gone his way.

So they searched the best they could, separating a little but keeping within easy sight of each other, and flashing their fights about in wide arcs.

They finally reached the line of firs which stretched beyond the Bowen property.

"What do you make of this?" Nelson demanded.

"Strange, very strange." Ted pondered. "You know we've always had the feeling this was an inside job. Look how the man went right to that skylight and dropped in, just as though he knew exactly what he was doing. But everybody around here knew about the poisonous spray and how deadly it could be, and it seems now that the intruder didn't. That means it couldn't have been an inside job."

"So where do we go from here?" Nelson asked impatiently.

"I see it this way, Nel. The dog has been seen before, the prowler has walked before. The howling was heard from the swamp. I believe that the dog and the man were together, and are still together, since we haven't found any trace of the dog, either. They must have some sort of shack out in the swamp, where they've been staying. He's out there, and he may be in serious trouble."

"What about the police?"

"They've got their hands full checking the roads. There's only a small country force here, you know. I don't like to wait."

"It's a strange swamp, Ted, and we don't have any idea where they are. What do we have to go on?"

"About the only thing I can think of is the direction we heard the dog howling."

"Just one thing, Ted. I know you don't want to go back to ask Mrs. B., because she'll say no, and you really think we ought to go. But let's at least leave a note for them in the cottage so they'll know where we went—and my social security card." He seemed obsessed with the idea he might lose it.

This was agreeable to Ted, and the note was written and placed on the kitchen table. The two boys set out, after replacing their weapons in the vestibule.

They retraced their steps to the point where they had heard the howling, and tried to agree where the sound had come from. It was finally decided it was off a little to their left.

"And anywhere from a quarter of a mile to half a mile away," was Nelson's opinion. "There was a light wind, you remember."

The fine of firs lay behind them. The tall grass was almost marshy, and undoubtedly concealed many a treacherous booby trap. It seemed most unlikely that even a person familiar with the woods would have risked a passage through there in the darkness.

"And quicksand," Nelson warned. "I'll bet there's some around. This has all the markings."

"We don't know how long he was in that fumigated greenhouse," Ted reviewed. "We know he went through the roof of the first building, found some way out on the opposite side of that house and into the fumigated house, and then went out the door. The whole thing must have taken between fifteen and twenty minutes, but we have no way of dividing it between the two greenhouses, so we don't know how badly off he might be, but I hate to wait till morning."

"I'd say that going through that marshland is the best way I know to collect on your insurance, but my neck isn't worth any more than yours," Nelson said.

"There ought to be a path," Ted decided. "I don't see how anyone could make it in the dark unless he had a path he was familiar with."

They walked a short way along the edge of the morass, until Ted pointed his flashlight sharply at a small object on the ground. It was a pocket pencil, and seemed to have been dropped quite recently, for there was no sign of weathering.

"I'll bet our man came this way, and this is the beginning of the path," Ted said.

"If it is, it was originally made by a rabbit," was Nelson's disgruntled answer, but no more promising path appeared nearby, and he was willing to try it.

"Let's stay a little distance apart," Ted suggested. "Then at least we won't both step into trouble at the same time."

"All right, if you let me go first."

"No, I'll go first. You're stronger than I am, and would have a better chance of pulling me out if I got stuck."

Nelson agreed, and Ted started down the faint path with Nelson a discreet distance behind. The moon was now low in the west, and the shadows it cast were long and barely distinctive in the general gloom. Occasionally there was a startled rustling in the leaves, and an owl that had been to Harvard flew off screaming, "Whom, whom, whom," its silhouette momentarily visible against the moon.

"I think we've lost the path, Ted," was Nelson's cheery comment.

"I think you're right," Ted agreed.

"Take it awfully, awfully easy," Nelson cautioned. "Isn't this ground getting soggy?"

"Sure is. Maybe we ought to go back."

But this advice was easier given than taken, for in following the elusive path they had made many turns, and no longer knew which way was back. Even the tall firs were now obscured by intervening trees. Nor did they have any idea how far they had come—perhaps only a quarter of a mile in a straight line, but their line was far from straight.

Ted struck off in a new direction, but this ground seemed just as uncertain as the other. Then he tried still another angle, and suddenly called warningly:

"Don't come any closer, Nel. My feet seem to be caught in the mud."

CHAPTER 13.

MOWGLI

WHETHER or not Ted was really caught in quicksand, there was no way to tell. It might be that he was stuck in thick mud, a few inches deep, from which he could easily extricate himself by freeing one leg at a time, and taking big steps back to safer ground. On the other hand, quicksand also frequently lay beneath a similar surface, a thick mixture of sand and water, replenished from some underground spring.

The proper thing was to throw yourself down so as to present as large a surface as possible to the mire, Ted knew. But he wasn't ready to surrender his best clothes to momentary panic.

"I'll toss you the end of my belt, Ted," Nelson said.

"No, don't do that. I don't want you to come that close. How about a long branch?"

"Okay. Don't go away."

He retreated a short distance to a nearby tree, and soon had a dead branch worked off. He then came back as close as he had been before. The branch was long enough, and Ted grasped it firmly. He had sunk a little deeper in. With the aid of the branch he was able to pull sufficiently to work his feet out, one step at a time, until he was at Nelson's side. He looked down. Only his shoes and the cuffs of his trousers had suffered. The ground was solid enough back to the tree, where Nelson suggested:

"Why don't we sit down here and wait till morning?"

Even to Ted this seemed the better part of wisdom. Suppose the man in the swamp still needed their help—what could they do about it? Their chance of finding him seemed more remote than ever.

"What's that?"

"Where?" Nelson followed Ted's indicating finger. "I don't see anything."

"It was a light. You can't see it now. The leaves have to blow just right."

Then another fresh gust of wind came along, and Nelson saw it, too.

"It looks like a shack to me, and not very far away. We weren't too much off the track after all. Still, the important thing is, what's between here and there? It might be more of that thick mud or quicksand."

They decided to take a bead on the light, and head straight toward it. If at any time the ground seemed too treacherous, they would retreat back to this tree and sit there till morning.

"He must have built his shack somewhere where he could get to it okay, and the dog wouldn't be likely to wander off into something too much to handle," Ted reasoned.

They started with Ted in the lead, as before. Nelson tried carrying the branch for a while, but it soon became too difficult to get through the brush, and he discarded it. However, the ground remained reasonably firm, and they advanced with growing confidence.

Then suddenly the shack came into view. It was small, and there was no window, but a light showed around the cracks in the door. They went up to it, expecting every minute that a dog would challenge them, but nothing happened. Getting Ted's nod of approval, Nelson knocked at the door. There was no answer, and a second knock was no more successful.

"Do we go in, Ted?"

"That's what we're here for. Watch out for the dog."

Nelson lifted the latch, and the door slowly opened. The room was indeed small, containing a cot, a table, and something that might have been called a fireplace if one were in a generous mood. The cot was occupied by a man, who made no gesture of any kind toward them, and on the floor at the head of the cot lay an enormous dog, his eyes glowing at them with the reflected light of the flickering lamp.

The dog was making no move toward them. He was there, alert, and would make his own move in his own time.

"I think he's smart enough to know we're here to help his master, not to hurt him," Nelson said. He talked soothingly to the dog, who made no response, but at least did nothing threatening as Ted advanced cautiously to the side of the bed. He bent over the reclining man.

It was clear to him at once that this man was not simply asleep. His breathing was forced, and he gave an occasonal little moan of half-consciousness. Ted looked under one eyelid, but found no recognition there.

"We'd better get help, Nel, right away. This is something I'm sure can't wait till morning."

"All right, I'll go. Unless you think we both ought to."

"There may be something I can do here for him. If his breathing stops, he'll need artificial respiration. I can leave the door open and the light will help you get back. But Nel, how are you going to find your way?"

"Down the path. It's much better marked here. I really don't think I'll have much trouble. In fact I think I'm safer than you." He gestured toward the unblinking dog.

"If you can't get back, whistle," Ted advised. "One whistle if you need help, two whistles if you make it all right out of the swamp."

Nelson left with the brighter of the two flashlights, and Ted watched him until he disappeared into the foliage. Then he turned back to give his attention to the victim. This was a young man, bearded, poorly clothed, certainly no one that Ted recognized. His face was gaunt, as though he had not had enough to eat for a long time.

The young man's breathing was no better than before, but no worse, either. There was nothing Ted could do for him at the moment, and he turned away, listening at the door for Nelson's whistle. Then it came, one whistle, followed by another. Nelson had made it all right—and fortunately hadn't lost his pucker after the first whistle.

With nothing to do but wait, Ted gave some attention to the dog, whose eyes followed his every movement. Otherwise he lay perfectly still. This wasn't the sort of dog you could make up to; he was undoubtedly a one-man dog, well trained and reserved. Ted patted his own side with his hand to indicate friendliness, but the dog wasn't buying.

Time passed slowly, with Ted keeping his eyes on both the man and the dog. Then, through the open door, he heard people coming. The dog pricked up his ears, but made no other sign. When they arrived, Nelson was accompanied by two men in white uniforms, carrying a stretcher and a medical kit.

"Does that dog bite?" asked the intern.

"He hasn't so far," was Ted's answer.

"Well, keep an eye on him." Then the intern bent over the unconscious man, and examined him, as Ted watched the dog. He felt that any movement of the dog to leap would be betrayed by a telltale growling or tensing of muscles, but the dog lay there unmoving, plainly confused by his unresponsive master. He had been trained to obedience, and now there was no one to obey.

The intern straightened up and put away his stethoscope. "This is all I can do for him here. Better get him onto the stretcher and to the hospital as quickly as possible."

The two men reached for the patient to place him on the litter, and for the first time the dog got to his feet. Now, if ever, he was going to make his move.

Stopping the dog was easier said than done, since Ted had no idea what might antagonize him. The only thing he could think of to do was to stand between the dog and the men, but this seemed the most likely thing to rile him. So Ted stood off a little, not barring his vision.

The men carried their patient to the door and outside, and the dog began to follow slowly.

"What should we do with him?" asked Nelson.

"Shut him in the cabin. We can't fool around with him. This may be a matter of life and death."

The dog had hesitated just inside the door, and now Nelson drew the door firmly closed, the dog inside, the lamp still burning. If the animal resented this move, he made no outcry.

As Nelson had predicted, the path, at least at this end, was well marked. Nelson led the way with a lantern, and Ted made up the rear with a flashlight. They walked swiftly, considering the terrain, and were soon out of the swamp.

An ambulance, its light flashing bright red, was waiting for them not far from the cottage. Several persons from the estate had gathered there, and watched as the patient was put into the vehicle.

"Coming along?" the intern inquired, and Ted and Nelson stepped into the rear compartment, in case they could answer questions for the police.

There was no need for a siren on that lightly-traveled road, and they made good progress. In a short time they were at the hospital, and the patient was hurried inside. Ted and Nelson were referred to a doctor, who had asked to talk with them.

"They phoned already from the greenhouse to tell us what kind of poison he inhaled, so we know the score on that. Can you tell me anything else about his medical history?"

Ted shook his head. "He's a complete stranger to us. We never met him before tonight."

"That so? Can you refer me to anyone else who would know him?"

But the boys shook their heads again.

"I suppose you at least know his name?" but once again the boys were obliged to confess their ignorance. Shaking his own head, the doctor left them for a few minutes, then returned. "Well, that wasn't much help, either. There is no identification on him. Taking his fingerprints might be the first logical step. Would you boys mind waiting? The police will be along presently."

He left, and they seated themselves, until a police officer came into the room.

"I understand there's a difficulty over identification. Do you know anything at all about him?"

"Nothing that is likely to be of much use," Ted replied. "He evidently has been living in a hut in the swamp, with a large wolf-like dog, but for how long we have no idea."

"And just what sort of criminal activities has he been up to?"

"We don't know of anything for sure, except that of entering the greenhouses without permission after dark."

The officer asked: "You have no idea what he was after?"

Ted hesitated. It seemed probable that this man had entered the greenhouses for the purpose of going into the office safe and placing forged pages in the ledger. But this was such an absurd story to tell, and he had no proof anyway that this was the man responsible. He shook his head again.

"I couldn't say. It might be better for you to talk to Mr. or Mrs. Bowen."

"I'll do that, but I think it can wait till morning. We've had a wide alarm out for this man, and at least we can call that off and everybody can get home and get some sleep. Will you be around here if I want you again?"

"I'm working at the greenhouses for a few weeks," Nelson informed him.

"And if I'm not here, you can reach me at the *Town Crier* in Forestdale," Ted added.

The officer was about to leave, when the doctor returned.

"The patient regained consciousness, long enough to tell us that his name is Andy Brown. Does the name mean anything to you?"

Both boys shook their heads, and he went on, "One other thing, he said, 'Be sure to take care of Mowgli.' Do you have any idea what he meant?"

"He must mean his dog," Ted decided.

"Where is the dog now?"

"Shut in his shack in the woods."

"Will you be able to do something with him? My concern is for my patient, and I want to be able to reassure him in case he becomes disturbed about it."

"I suppose we could," Ted agreed. "I don't like to leave him out there very long anyway. Is there some place around here where we can board a dog?"

"Oh, yes," the officer said. "There's a kennel not far from Lutz. We'll pass it on our way back—that is, if you go with me. You don't have a car?"

"No, we rode in the ambulance."

"Then you may as well ride with me."

They were soon back at Lady Bee's, and the officer let them off on the side near the cottage.

"Sure you can handle that dog without me?"

"I guess we can handle him as well as anyone," said Ted with more confidence than he felt. "He knows us a little."

"And no trouble with the swamp?"

"No, now that we know the path," Nelson answered.

"Well, then, if you're sure it's all right to leave you, I'll get back home. I've been on duty for thirteen straight hours."

They were soon at the shack, but now it was completely dark, the lamp having burned itself out. They hesitated about opening the door, still uncertain about the conduct of the dog. But there was nothing to do but summon their courage and plunge in, so Nelson threw it open. Two eyes glowed at them as he turned the flashlight on the corner, but there was no sound.

"Here, Mowgli, here, Mowgli," Ted called him.

The name must have struck a familiar note, for the dog came slowly toward them.

"Ought we to tie him or something?" Nelson wondered.

" 'Who will bell the cat?' " Ted quoted. "No, I think he'll follow us now. He's confused, and is trying to make some sense out of things. Most of all he wants his master, and he may figure out that we are the best bet for that."

The dog followed them down the path, without further urging. Back near the cottage, Nelson hesitated once more.

"I don't think we ought to take him back to the parking lot. There are still people around, and I'm sure as shootin' that Mowgli isn't going to be friendly to everybody. Why don't we cut across down to the road, Ted, and then I can get my car and pick you up?"

This seemed the best course of action, and was accomplished quickly. Nelson left them, and was soon back with his car. He threw the back door open, and called to the dog to get in. The dog hesitated, then did so. Ted got in the front, but kept partly turned around to watch the dog.

They arrived at the dog kennel, managed to make them-selves heard without arousing the whole kennel, and Mowgli was soon placed in competent hands.

Nelson gave brief explanations, paid a deposit, and the boys drove off, more than ready to hit the hay.

CHAPTER 14.

VANDALISM

THOUGH the boys went to sleep promptly, they were not to enjoy an uninterrupted sleep. The next thing Ted knew, a flashlight was being turned into his face. He didn't know whether to be startled or annoyed, until the flashlight was turned in another direction and he saw who was behind it. It was Mr. Bowen.

"So there you are!" he exclaimed.

"Where did you think we were?" Nelson demanded irritably.

"Lost in the swamp. We've still got parties out looking for you."

It was difficult for Ted and Nelson to figure out why anyone would think they were lost in the swamp, for the only trouble they had had was many hours ago, and it was almost daylight now.

"Why were we supposed to be lost in the swamp?" asked Ted.

"You left a note saying you were going into the swamp, didn't you, and we had no certain word that you ever got out," Mr. Bowen replied.

"That was long, long ago," Nelson pointed out. "Didn't you know we were the ones who found that young man in the shack?"

"No. Somebody said he saw somebody like you with the ambulance crew, and somebody else said it wasn't you, and somebody else said he saw the two of you going into the swamp later. And of course we checked the cottage and found the note. It did seem if you had come back you would at least have destroyed the note. Your car was still in the lot, too, when we checked."

"I came back just for a moment to make a telephone call for the ambulance, and I was too worried to think about a note then. Then we went to the hospital in the ambulance, and back into the swamp again for the dog and took him to the kennel, and by the time we got back we were too tired to think of anything."

"I'd suggest calling your families the first thing in the morning."

"Why our families?"

"Because they'll be worried. Naturally, when I thought you were lost in the swamp I called Mr. Dobson, and no doubt he notified your families."

"Yipes!" Nelson jumped up as though he'd been lying on a nettle. "There won't be any more sleep for my mother till she hears from us."

"Mine either," Ted agreed, also jumping up. "I'll call my mother, and she can call yours."

"No, I'd better talk to her myself."

The calls were made and parents reassured, and then the boys finally got back to bed again. The early morning sun aroused Ted, and though he would have relished a few more hours' sleep, he decided to get up before he gave in to temptation. Nelson heard him as he brushed his shoes, trying without much success to get rid of the swamp mud.

"Why so early, Ted?"

"I'm thinking I'd better get back to Forestdale this morning. I'm still concerned about Brown, and curious about his story. And I've a couple of other things on my mind, too. I'll pick up that ledger from Professor Wiggins, and I want to stop again in Holiday."

"How come, Ted?"

"Well, Mr. Bowen knows more about his business than I do, and if he's interested in Holiday, I think I ought to be, too."

The walk across the estate to the parking lot was almost half the distance to the bus stop, but Nelson insisted on driving Ted to the bus stop. They went out together. As they approached the greenhouses, something startling struck their eyes. The door to the strong room seemed to have been broken in.

"Another burglary, Ted?"

"I don't know. Let's ask."

At the moment there didn't seem to be anyone to ask, but presently an employee showed up.

"What happened here?" asked Nelson.

"Why, we helped Mr. Bowen break in the door last night. They tried to get hold of Mr. Gompers, but he wasn't around, so Mrs. B. called some of the other employees to break in here, and then help search for the young man. I don't know whom we were looking for. Was it one of you two?"

"Could be," Ted said, deciding that further explanations would only complicate things more. Mr. and Mrs. Bowen would do well to re-think this one-key gimmick; it could lead to serious complications.

He arrived at the *Town Crier* office before the usual opening time, and went right to work. His typewriter was clicking away as Carl arrived, less than five minutes early, as he always was.

"Well, so our wandering boy is home again."

"Where did you think I was?"

"The alarm was out that you were lost in the swamp, and the newspaper profession was in danger of losing a future Pulitzer Prize winner."

Ted looked up from the typewriter, and saw that Carl, who was usually immaculately dressed, looked as though he had slept in his clothes. "Where were *you?*"

"Out in the swamp, looking for a missing person. After I heard he was found, it was too late to get a room, so I got a few hours' sleep in my car."

"Why did you go to all that bother?" Ted was touched.

"You know I wouldn't want you to drown. Somebody might think I pushed you in."

Ted spent two hours typing Carl's stories, and turned them over to him for his inspection.

"Oh, Ted, you know a man named Tony Thorton?"

"Yes, he works at Lady Bee's."

"He was a member of our searching party last night. He didn't seem to recognize me, although I've met him before. But not under that name, or at least that was only one of his names. I attended his trial."

"His trial? For what?"

"For forgery and related offenses. I was surprised to see him out so soon."

Ted almost jumped, though he tried to appear calm. Suddenly some things were becoming clear to him. Undoubtedly Mrs. Bowen had known of Thorton's past record, and that was the reason she was so upset at the discovery of the forgeries.

"Was that his first offense?"

"I very much doubt it," said Carl, "but it was his first conviction. I don't know what you're onto down there, Ted, but I thought the tip might help you."

"It sure does, Carl. Thanks a lot."

Obviously there was no use telling Mrs. Bowen about Thorton, since she already knew it. But what in the world were they supposed to do about the man, and was it any of Ted's business or was it strictly a problem for the Bowens? He was still puzzling over the matter when a call came for him.

"Ted? This is Mrs. King. If you're not too busy, could you come over right away?"

"I'll be right there, Mrs. King." He hung up without waiting to ask her what was wrong. After telling Miss Monroe where he was going, he hurried out of the office.

Mrs. King was waiting for him in her front yard. Without a word she led him around to the back. Her beautiful rose garden looked as though it had been the victim of a stampede. Not a single rose bush was left standing. Every stalk was broken, and further, the blossoms and branches were crushed into the ground. Rose petals were strewn everywhere.

"What a shame!" Ted exclaimed, torn between pity and a fighting rage. "Whoever it was made a pretty thorough job of it. Did you hear anything, Mrs. King?"

"No, we were not at home. We were attending a wedding reception, and of course we didn't get home until late. My husband left his car in the drive, and we went directly into the house without going anywhere near the garden. Then I looked out this morning, and this is what I saw." Her voice choked.

"I'll certainly put something about this in the *Town Crier,* Mrs. King, though I don't suppose it will do any good." He thought dully how thorough a disaster it was for Mrs. King, since this would end her participation in the rose show. "I'm awfully sorry about Blue Lady."

"Oh, you needn't be sorry about that, Ted. It is the one thing *not* to be sorry about. Come, I'll show you." She opened the back door, and he stepped into the kitchen. She went directly to the refrigerator, opened it, and took out a plastic-wrapped package. "Here is my Blue Lady."

"It is? How did you happen to do a thing like that?"

"Well, I knew we were going to be out very late, and the weather report spoke of thunderstorms. Normally show flowers are cut on the day preceding the show, but I didn't think it would hurt to cut them a day early, as long as they were refrigerated properly."

"You were certainly lucky, Mrs. King. I'm very happy for you."

At noon Ted returned home for a quick lunch, and then caught the bus again for Lutz. He found Nelson about to climb a ladder for the greenhouse roofs.

"I'm learning a lot about greenhouse work, Ted, the kinds of soil and how to prepare beds and loads of things. Mrs. B. has hopes of making a gardener out of me—at least a hobby gardener."

Then Ted told Nelson about the forger, probably on parole, and Nelson was just as startled as Ted had been.

"Where is Tony Thorton today, Nel?"

"He never showed up for work."

"I suppose that's understandable, if he was up a good part of the night in the swamp."

"Mrs. B. asked about him. She thought that at least he would call in. She phoned the boarding house where he has a room, but he wasn't there. She did mention that he had a brother somewhere in the area, but she didn't know how to reach him. Do you suppose, Ted, that Tony Thorton recognized Carl, and that made him decide to vamoose?"

"Either that, or he decided things were getting too hot for him anyway."

Then Mrs. Bowen came over to them, and Ted told the tale of the vandalism.

"What a pity! I shall certainly see if I can't do something about helping her to replace her garden."

"It might give you a chance to see her Blue Lady, too," Ted suggested.

"Why, yes, that would give me an appropriate excuse. I might even take Governor Hope along, and we could compare them point by point. Anything we can work out in private would save that much washing of dirty linen in public."

Mr. Bowen came along to join them. "I've just come from the police station, and I'm sure you will want to know that Andy Brown is going to be all right."

"I'm so glad to hear that," said Mrs. Bowen.

"But what was his angle?" asked Nelson.

"Well, it's a strange story, but maybe not so strange, considering the times we live in. Andy Brown is about thirty years old, and one of these typical beatnik types—a beard and old clothes and I wouldn't be surprised if he has bongo drums tucked away somewhere. He hadn't been out in the swamp very long, and I don't know how long he intended to stay."

"What explanation did he give for breaking into the greenhouse?" Ted inquired.

"According to the police, he thinks he owns the world, or at least he owns it as much as anybody else does. He doesn't recognize that these greenhouses belong to us."

"What do you plan to do about him?" asked Ted.

"Oh, I don't know. He's had a very narrow escape, and maybe that will teach him something, if anything can. Under the circumstances I don't feel like pressing charges, at least not a simple trespassing charge, unless we could prove something else against him. Perhaps, if he really liked flowers, we could offer him a job here—"

"Save your sympathy. I think a job is the last thing in the world he wants."

CHAPTER 15.

TONY THORTON'S BROTHER

WITH Nelson returning to his glazing ladders, Ted took his car and set off for the university.

When Professor Wiggins handed him the ledger and his report, he pointed out: "You realize, Ted, that these forgeries are high-class work? I thought it best to warn you that there is a professional forger at work here somewhere."

"Yes, I know," said Ted unhappily, "but I don't know what to do about it."

"I've run into a good many queer cases, but I must admit I've never heard of forgeries in connection with papers like this. Well, there's something new turning up every day. If you could get me a sample of handwriting from anyone you suspect, I should be able to tell whether or not he is the forger. Good luck with the case, Ted."

"Thank you, Professor."

On the way home Ted drove slowly into and out of Holiday. It seemed to him that if Mr. Bowen had really spent last weekend there, he probably stayed in a motel. A mile outside of Holiday he saw one which seemed to be a likely spot. He turned into the lot, got out, and went into the office.

"I'm wondering if a friend of mine stopped in here last Saturday and Sunday nights."

The clerk turned to the register. "What was his name?"

"Bowen."

"Oh, yes, he was a guest here both nights. You know his address, of course."

"Yes, the Lady Bee Floral Nursery near Lutz. I'll contact him there."

"If you're interested in nurseries, maybe you'd be interested in our own local project. Did you notice our new greenhouse?"

"Yes, I did. Has it been here long?"

"For several years. If you want to see it, I'm sure Mr. Player, the superintendent will show you around."

As Ted drove off, he realized that Mr. Bowen hadn't pulled the name Holiday out of thin air, but had actually been there on the days specified. His purpose was undoubtedly connected with the greenhouse. It might not be a bad idea to talk to Mr. Player, the manager, according to a sign. After all . . . Mr. Player? The name began to sound familiar. Then it came to Ted: it was Mrs. Tolman's former neighbor, the one who had given her Blue Lady! His excitement grew.

He returned to the greenhouse drive and parked. He inquired of one of the nearby employees, who directed him to a man with an intent expression stooping over a row of shrubs.

"Mr. Player?" The superintendent straightened up. "I'm Ted Wilford of the Forestdale *Town Crier.* The newspaper is interested in the Loki Pageant of Roses, and while I was here I wondered whether you were planning to participate."

Mr. Player shook his head. "Afraid not. We're a long way from that."

"It's odd, Mr. Player, but—there's something else. Did you once live in Winter's Ledge?"

"Yes, I did. Then I found a position managing this greenhouse, so I moved out into this area."

"Well, then, we have an acquaintance in common. Mrs. Tolman. She told me that you gave her a rose, which she gave to her sister, and it turned out so well that it is being entered in the pageant."

"That so? I'm really very pleased to hear that, Wilford. It was a cull, you know. I'm glad it worked out."

Quite evidently he did not remember this particular flower, and Ted thought it best not to go into too much detail. A valuable plant like this, given away as a cull, would have to be a mistake of some kind.

Though Mr. Player offered to show him around, Ted was pressed for time, so after a few perfunctory questions, Ted thanked him and left. If Blue Lady and Governor Hope were the same, Ted felt that he had established a route from the Holiday greenhouse to Mr. Player to Mrs. Tolman to Mrs. King. The remaining link lay between Lady Bee's and the Holiday operation, and this was something Tony Thorton might be able to explain, if he could be located. If it was true he had a brother nearby, that might be the quickest approach to the problem. But even Mrs. Bowen had said she didn't know how to locate the brother, so it was apparent that the problem was more difficult than simply looking up the name in the telephone book.

He stopped in the next town and inquired at a drug store for a directory, turned to the T's, but there was no Thorton listed.

He continued to consider the problem on the remainder of his trip. A brother in the area . . . how close an area? It was perhaps the brother who had helped Tony Thorton get his job at the greenhouse.

What was in the area, anyway? Small stores, service stations, farms . . . hardly anything in the way of an industry, except the chemical lab, and that was by no means a large place. Still, was it worth trying? Chances were he wasn't set up in business for himself, or Mrs. Bowen would know where to find him.

Ted stopped in Lutz and put in a call to the lab, hoping they were not already closed. When the switchboard girl answered, he asked for Mr. Thorton.

"I'm sorry, there is no Mr. Thorton here."

Another dead end. He was about to thank her and hang up, when a highly improbable idea occurred to him. You expect brothers to have the same last name, but it doesn't always happen. Sometimes one of them has changed his name.

"Then could you connect me with Mr. Thorton's brother?"

If you dig often enough you'll find gold eventually, and this time he struck pay dirt. There was a short conversation in the background that he could not understand, and then a man's voice came on.

"Yes?"

"Are you Mr. Thorton's brother?"

"Which Mr. Thorton?"

"Tony Thorton."

"Oh." The man seemed to be digesting the information.

"Who are you?"

"I'm Ted Wilford, a reporter for the Forestdale *Town Crier*."

"A reporter, eh? What have you dug up now? Well, I suppose the best thing I can do is to talk to you, but I can't talk now. How about in an hour?"

"Fine," Ted agreed. "Where?"

"I forgot, you don't even know my name. I can't imagine where you reporters get your information, but sometimes it must be from the devil himself. My name's Cowling, and I live on River Road just before you cross the bridge."

"Thank you, Mr. Cowling. I'll be there."

The man hung up with a grunt.

After dinner Ted and Nelson drove out to River Road together, located the house, and were admitted into the living room.

"Well, now?" Mr. Cowling began when they were seated. It was apparent that he hoped to get more information than he intended to give.

"Mr. Cowling," Ted began, "do you know where your brother is?"

"I can't see that that is a question I have to answer one way or the other."

"He stole a bundle of rose clippings from Mrs. Bowen. He forged some records. He probably stole a tank of poisonous spray. And he has broken his parole. Is that enough for you?"

"You seem to know a good deal about my brother. Suppose he did do these things. What do you expect me to do?"

"Turn him in," Nelson answered. "He has broken his parole, hasn't he?"

Mr. Cowling, obviously, was not going to discuss his brother's parole status. "Just in case I could get a message to him, what would be the nature of that message?"

"Why," said Ted, "I suppose the only thing is—not to get in any deeper."

"He does have a little sense of his own, you know, and I doubt that he needs advice from strangers. However, I will assume that your intentions are good, and give him the message, if I get the opportunity."

He stood up in dismissal, and they were soon outside and on their way again, wondering what, if anything, they had accomplished.

CHAPTER 16.

CAPTURE

WHY don't we stop at the hospital and ask about Andy Brown?" Ted suggested.

"All right, Ted, for whatever good it might do."

When they inquired at the desk, the nurse consulted her file, and said, "Your names?"

"Ted Wilford and Nelson Morgan."

"Then I have a note for you. Doctor Haines has barred other visitors, but he said that you were to be admitted. The patient has asked for you. You may go up immediately. Room 336."

As they rode up in the elevator, Ted remarked, "I suppose he wants to ask us about his dog."

They found the room and stepped through the open doorway. At first they thought they had made a mistake, for the young man on the bed certainly had no beard. He was neat and friendly, and almost certainly less than the thirty years he was supposed to be.

"Andy Brown?" Ted stepped forward and extended his hand.

"You must be Ted and Nelson. Which is which?" This was straightened out for him, and he went immediately to the point. "Now about my dog."

"He's at a kennel near Lutz, and was in good shape when we delivered him there last night."

"There must have been a fee. Who paid it?" When Nelson nodded, he went on, "I'll pay you back as soon as I get a chance."

Suddenly Ted laughed. "Nel, we know this young man."

"We do?" He studied the patient for a moment. "No, I don't think I ever saw him before."

"No? Well, try again. You may not have seen him, but you know a relative of his."

Nelson looked again, and his eyes widened. "Why, it's Mrs. Bowen. That's the shape of her cheek and jawbone. You must be her son."

"Yes, I'm Buzz Bowen," the young man admitted.

"Well, what's with all this beatnik jazz?"

"No jazz, at least not at first. Of course it made a good disguise."

"I heard that you were away at college," Ted said.

"I had two years of junior college. That was enough for me. I'm not a scholar. But I didn't want to go home again. I had a quarrel with my parents. It was mostly that they took it for granted I would enter the nursery business. It wasn't such a bad plan; it was just that is wasn't *my* plan. This is the atomic age, the jet age, the space age, and here were my parents, growing roses just the way they might have done a hundred years ago! Naturally they objected to my plans, or lack of plans, as they called it. I'm afraid harsh things were said, mostly by me.

"So I headed out on my own. No matter what I was doing, something else always looked a little better to me. So I skipped around a lot, and never stuck long to anything. I was always looking for the place the action was, and when I got there I found the action wasn't very much anyway.

"All that will be of interest to you is my latest caper. I was driving one day in my car with a friend. He was at the wheel, and wrapped my car around a utility pole, and it bounced off and rammed a parked car—and there were people sitting in the car.

"It was a miracle we weren't hurt, although the car was a wreck. Just before we got out he said, 'You'd better say you were driving. I don't have a license. It's suspended.' We crawled out of the car and I pretended I had been driving. 'Thanks, pal,' he told me in a whisper, and that was the last I ever saw of him!

"I owed some money on the car, and the company had only the balance due insured, so the rest of the loss was mine. I wasn't carrying any liability insurance, because that state didn't require it, and you know what the rates are in our age bracket. I don't think those people in the parked car were really hurt at all, but they had a sharp lawyer. They wanted damages from me, and hinted if I didn't come through there might be criminal charges instead. There was some publicity about it in the newspaper, which was carrying on a safety campaign, and I lost my job. I was flat broke, and faced with the prospect of making an extravagant settlement on a civil suit or facing criminal charges.

"There was only one place I could think of to get the money. As a boy my parents paid me for my work around the greenhouses, and the money went into a savings account to pay for my college. I only had two years of college, so there was quite a sum left, perhaps enough to make a settlement with that lawyer. It was really my money, wasn't it?

"Mowgli and I needed some place to stay, so I thought of this shack in the swamp. Furthermore, I knew of Mother's habit of keeping the refrigerator stocked in the cottage, so Mowgli and I could at least get a little something to eat. I just about had bus fare to take us home."

"You did enter the cottage that night and steal the salami, didn't you?" asked Nelson, with an accusing look at Ted.

"Yes. Don't think the locks bothered me any. On one of the windows the putty is worn, and I could lift out the whole pane of glass."

"What about these trips through the greenhouses?" asked Ted. "What were you after?"

"Mother used to keep my savings book in the office safe. I went into it one night to see if it was there, but apparently she didn't keep it there any longer."

"What about the burglar alarm?"

"That didn't cramp my style any. I was there when they installed it, and knew where every wire was. And then, I had learned lots of ways to get in and out of the greenhouses, ventilators where the lock didn't always catch, things like that.

"I was curious about Mother's flowers, too, wondering what she had on the fire this time. I knew where she kept her prized treasures, and I looked them over. Sometimes the moonlight was bright enough; sometimes I risked a small light. Then, early one morning I saw this man—"

"Mr. Gompers?" Ted inquired.

"Oh, no, I know *him.* It was someone I didn't know—a thin, middle-aged man who walks with a kind of slouch."

"Tony Thorton," Nelson explained.

"Well, I saw him break into the strong room and take out a tank and put it in Mr. Gompers' car trunk. Of course I knew he had no right at all to do such a thing, so there was something up. After that I kept my eyes open, but I wasn't able to pinpoint anything."

"Didn't you know about the poisonous spray?"

"No, I didn't. You see, Mother was always dead set against such things when I was there. When I dropped into the greenhouse I smelled the fumigant, of course, but didn't figure it could be anything very bad, and maybe I just wasn't used to it. But I wasn't in there long before I realized I had to get out of there fast, and I headed straight for the nearest door, burglar alarm or no.

"I did manage to get back to the shack, and that was about all. Thanks for helping Mowgli."

"That's some dog," said Nelson, half envious. "There's been kind of a werewolf story going around here. Someone claimed to see you walk through the greenhouse wall, but we realize now you simply opened a ventilator. Anyway I'm glad Mowgli likes salami."

A little silence fell over the group, until Ted asked, "What do you want to do now?"

"I want to come home, and make something of myself in the nursery business . . . only this isn't the way I had planned to come home at all."

"If you were to come home, Buzz, I think your mother would consider it the most wonderful thing that ever happened to her. When do you get out of here?"

"Tomorrow afternoon, if I pass my examination."

"I suppose your mother will be on her way to Loki by then."

"Say, that's an idea. Why don't I go up to Loki and meet her there? That way there won't be all those private tears and remorse and maybe arguments and all that sort of thing. All you have to do is steal me some clothes."

"Huh?" exclaimed Nelson.

"Steal?" added Ted.

"Why, sure, you don't think I want to meet Mother in those old rags, do you? I'm sure she's still got all my clothes hanging in my closet. This is the conservatory hour, and you could get into the house. They never bother locking up during the day."

"What if we get caught?" asked Ted.

"Then I suppose you'd have to tell the truth, but don't *get* caught. Tomorrow how about driving me to Loki?"

"All right," Nelson agreed reluctantly.

They drove back to Lady Bee's, and parked almost in front of the Bowen home. It had been agreed that Nelson would go on to the conservatory, and if Mr. and Mrs. Bowen were there, he would give Ted a signal, and Ted would go into the house. Then Ted would drive to the hospital alone.

Ted received a kind of tentative signal from Nelson, decided it was the right one, and got out of the car. There was a door in the Bowen house on the side away from the greenhouses, and Ted decided to try that. It opened, and he went inside. Following the directions Buzz had given him, he went upstairs, found Buzz's suit on a hanger, and packed a suitcase for him with shoes, shirts, and other things. Then he hurried downstairs and outside. He looked around to see if anyone had seen him, and there, looking directly at him, was Miss Lance.

It would be silly to pretend not to see her, and all he could think to say was, "Good evening," which made him feel as foolish as he had ever felt in his life. Miss Lance did not reply, and continued to watch him as he got into the car and drove off.

He delivered the clothes to a nurse at the hospital, and made up his mind that his first experience at house-breaking was also going to be his last.

As night fell and the grounds became deserted, Ted and Nelson were out on the estate again, from their hiding place behind the hedge watching for sabotage of Governor Hope, because of the vandalism in Mrs. King's garden.

"Think we ought to alert Mr. Bowen to help us?" asked Ted.

"Can't. He's out of town for the evening. Didn't you get my signal? It meant I wasn't sure where he was, but thought it was all right."

Ted groaned. "Now you tell me. Whatever we do we had better do tonight, because after Miss Lance tells Mrs. Bowen, we'll get our walking papers."

It must have been nearly midnight when they suddenly saw a man in the moonlight. He walked directly to one of the doors, opened it, and went inside. The burglar alarm startled them with its silence.

"This must be a real pro," Nelson whispered. "He knows how to disconnect the alarm. What do we do, go after him?"

"We tried waiting last time, and it didn't work. There are too many places to come out, and we aren't sure he'll come back the same way. Yes, let's try going after him this time. Wasn't that a flash of light?"

"I saw it, but it didn't look like a flashlight, Ted."

"No. I'll bet he opened the door to the Fun House. They've probably got light on in there."

Quickly the boys hurried to the door the man had entered and went inside. They were still in possible trouble from the burglar alarm, since they didn't know just which parts had been disconnected, but they went on anyway. If the alarm rang, they might be no worse off.

They approached the door to the Fun House, and cautiously opened it. They could see no one in the lighted room, but thought they heard the closing of a door on the other side.

"In the orchid room," Nelson whispered. "Think he heard us coming?"

"I think he did, and that's why he got out of here. Come on."

And now they could hear running feet, so they knew there was no longer need for secrecy. They raced through the darkened orchid room and out the other side into one of the regular long rooms. They heard a scuffling down a long aisle, and ran in pursuit of the noise. Someone was up there ahead of them, running as though he knew the place well. They followed, then listened, and heard the scuffling sound again, down another aisle, going in the opposite direction.

They ran in the direction of the sound, but up ahead they heard a door open and saw a man in the doorway; then he was gone. They followed, and as Nelson put his hand on the door handle he exclaimed: "There's something sticky on here! It feels like blood. He must have cut himself in his hurry to open the door."

They went outside and looked around, but there was no one in sight.

"We've lost him again," said Nelson.

"No, I'm not so sure we lost him," Ted said. "Come on."

He led the way to the opposite side of the Bowen home, and suggested that they hide behind some low shrubs.

"What goes, Ted?" Nelson whispered. "Think he's going to rob the Bowen's house?"

"It's my hunch this is his next stop. Let's wait and see."

Half an hour later a car drew up into the drive and a man got out. Ted stood up, and walked boldly up to him.

"Good evening, Mr. Bowen. I see you cut your hand."

"On the greenhouse door," Nelson added.

Saying, "I'll see you in the morning, boys," Mr. Bowen went into the house.

"All right, Ted," said Nelson grimly, "I've seen you pull a rabbit out of a hat, and I don't know how you did it. How did you know it was Mr. Bowen we were chasing?"

"Oh, that. The burglar alarm was off, wasn't it? Who would have shut it off except Mr. Bowen? Come on, I want to make a telephone call."

At the cottage, Ted phoned Mr. Cowling.

"Could you add something to my previous message to your brother? Tell him we now have a pretty good inkling why he did the things he did."

"All right, Ted, I'll be sure to do that. Thanks a lot." And they hung up.

CHAPTER 17.

THE SECRET OF HOLIDAY

THE group met next morning in the Bowens' living room. Present were Mr. and Mrs. Bowen, Ted and Nelson, and—to the Bowens' complete surprise—Tony Thorton. The Bowens looked expectantly to Ted.

"I know you think I've asked for this meeting because I've figured something out. Well, I have figured some things, and other things I haven't. But I do feel that each of us here has some information, and if we were all to pool our information, we might be able to solve this whole thing. Is everybody willing?"

Mr. and Mrs. Bowen and Mr. Thorton all nodded their heads.

Then Ted said: "Perhaps you would care to begin, Mrs. Bowen."

"I'm not sure I understand, Ted. About what?"

"About Tony Thorton."

She looked uncertain. "Are you sure you want me to, Mr. Thorton?"

"Yes, please go ahead, Mrs. Bowen. You've been very considerate of me—gave me the chance that not very many people would have—and now I might be in a position to return the favor."

"Well, then, apparently this is no secret to Ted and Nelson, and so the only person in the dark about it is my husband." She turned to him. "I may as well tell you that Tony Thorton is on parole from the state penitentiary."

Mr. Bowen looked startled. "Why didn't you tell me before?"

"Because you are such a *reasonable* person, and I felt that this was one time where I had to trust my intuition."

"In other words, you were afraid I might talk you out of it. Were you under any obligation to this man?"

"None at all. I never met him until he came to work here."

"Then as I understand it, you were asked to give employment to a complete stranger who had served a term in the state penitentiary. No wonder you didn't want to talk to me about it!"

"If I might amplify the situation, Mr. Bowen," said Thorton, "here's how the thing stands. A parolee can't get out of the pen unless he has the offer of a job. But who is going to hire an ex-convict, if he can get another man? People like Mrs. Bowen are one in a million."

"What was your crime, Mr. Thorton?"

"Forgery."

"Forgery!" If Mr. Bowen had looked startled before, he was now twice as amazed. "Did you have any particular aptitude for this job, Mr. Thorton?"

"Oh, yes. I worked in the gardens while in prison. My best aptitude is for desk work, but they thought it better to get me into a different field."

Mr. Bowen seemed about to say something more, but Ted interrupted:

"And now, Mr. Bowen, I think it would be appropriate for you to contribute your share."

"About what, Ted?"

"About where you spent last weekend."

It was Mrs. Bowen's turn to look surprised. "Weren't you in jail?"

"No, dear, I was not. I'm sorry if I needlessly aroused your sympathies. You must have done some detective work, Ted. What put you onto it?"

"Simply that there isn't any jail in Holiday."

He smiled. "That so? It never occurred to me, since I felt any inhabited place would have a jail of some sort. Since you know I wasn't in jail, Ted, I presume you know where I was—and why."

"I know you spent the weekend in Holiday. I assume there was something about the greenhouse there that attracted you, something you wanted to investigate."

"All true enough, Ted. I did feel it was an odd set-up. Some of my customers, I found, had purchased things from this new greenhouse. Well, all right, they're not under contract to us, and are free to buy elsewhere when they like. But naturally I was curious about a possible new competitor of ours.

"But I was suspicious about the particular items offered for sale. The company seemed to have no specialty of its own, none of its own patented roses or such things to attract trade. But I did notice that what they did have seemed to parallel our own stock a good deal. It began to seem that what they had to offer was a smaller selection than ours—but the best that we had. You could believe that they had selected their stock from ours.

"I was especially struck by the fact that they had out-of-season 'mums, and other such plants, where it did not seem to me that they had facilities for light-controlled bloomings. That was the reason I was exploring our own Fun House last night, to see if anything had been disturbed."

"Did you find anything?" asked Ted.

"Nothing definite, but possible indications. All I can say is that the Holiday greenhouse still puzzles me, but I have no proof of anything. I certainly intend to continue my investigation—unless you can supply me with information that makes it unnecessary."

"I don't think I can, Mr. Bowen, but perhaps Mr. Thorton can. There is a possible route for Governor Hope from here to Holiday to Mrs. Tolman in Winter's Ledge to Mrs. King in Forestdale, where it turned up as Blue Lady. I have talked with Mr. Player at the Holiday greenhouse, and I am pretty sure that whatever is going on, he doesn't have anything to do with it. The fact that the manager of the Holiday greenhouse gave away this prize rose is evidence of that.

"Of one thing I feel sure—the guilty party certainly didn't want this lavender rose to appear on the market, and most especially did not want it to turn up at the Loki Pageant. While someone was prowling through the greenhouses Tuesday night, someone else was trampling Mrs. King's rose garden seventy-five miles away in Forestdale. It appeared at first to be merely a vicious kind of vandalism, but I think it was something more. Whoever was responsible had read in the *Town Crier* that morning about Mrs. King's intention to display the rose, and he couldn't afford to let that happen, in case it would be traced to him. That he trampled the whole garden may be due to the fact that he could not identify Blue Lady in the dark, or it may be that he did not want to destroy Blue Lady alone, for then it might be clear to someone just what he was after.

"And I don't think there is much doubt of what he is after—the patent to Governor Hope. I think that his patent application is already in, and he was anxious to get it approved before there was any publicity about a similar rose. Such a prestige item might help get his greenhouse operation off the ground. I do think, though, that Governor Hope was just one of a long series of thefts where he was helping himself to your best stock, many items not available elsewhere, many that you were not yet ready to market yourself. Since Governor Hope may have been stolen anytime from one to three years ago, depending upon just which stage of development it was in when stolen, this has been going on for a long time; but I think the thefts would have ended soon. Governor Hope would be his crowning achievement, and after these present experiments, he would transfer to his own operation, the greenhouse in Holiday, of which he was the secret owner.

"Naturally when you try to figure out who was behind all this, you suspect a person with a criminal record. But Mr. Thorton has been in jail for most of this period, so that would appear to eliminate him.

"And now we come to the theft of those Canadian cuttings. I had thought at first that these would be useless to the thief, and he merely intended to damage the Lady Bee Nursery. But now I can see where they might prove very useful to a developing nursery. As Mrs. Bowen said, it would be difficult for some other nursery to get similar clippings. There are international shipping regulations that are difficult to fulfill, and she also needed the cooperation of an expert friend in Canada.

"I believe the bundle of clippings left by the back door, in spite of the fumigation. If so, Mr. Thorton was the most obvious person to steal them, and a girl named Laurel claimed that she did indeed see him leaving the greenhouse after four o'clock, instead of three o'clock as he claimed. But obviously she just assumed that it was Mr. Thorton because she knew that he was the one who was fumigating—and the man was wearing a mask.

"I think Mr. Thorton had better explain about the forged pages in the daybook."

Tony Thorton fidgeted a little before beginning. "First of all, your safe is quite easy to open, and if you ever put anything really valuable in there, I'd suggest you get a better one. Now your strong room is a much more difficult proposition. The combination lock is a good one, and when you combine this with the need for a key, I think your protection is remarkably good. The fact that you gave me an opportunity to get a duplicate of the key made one time, by asking me to get it from Mr. Gompers, helped me immeasurably."

"Didn't the burglar alarm deter you?" asked Mr. Bowen, flabbergasted.

"Oh, yes. But it was a simple matter to arrive early at work one morning before anyone else was around. I knew the time the burglar alarm was shut off, went into the room before Mr. Gompers had arrived, took out the tank and concealed it until he came, and then put it in the trunk of his car. I never entered the office safe when the alarm was set, either."

"And you don't think your parole officer will be interested in such activities?" demanded Mr. Bowen.

"My sole motivation was to help Mrs. Bowen, in return for the break she gave me. If it had not been for her, I would still be in prison. Now when I was put to work in the prison garden, I learned my trade well. When I came out of prison, I knew considerably more than anyone thought I knew, and considerably more than I cared to let people know that I knew. For this reason Mr. Gompers made no special effort to hide from me certain things he was doing. He thought I wouldn't know the difference anyway. And what I learned was that the information he was putting down in the daybook was often completely erroneous. Of course many of his entries were right; he did not always have a suitable opportunity to falsify them.

"Since he was so clever about it, I didn't think it likely Mrs. Bowen would catch him at it. Maybe she wouldn't even look at these entries till a long time afterward, and then more reliance would be placed on the written records than upon her own recollections.

"For all I knew there was another Governor Hope in development, and he was stealing it from her. He was getting all the benefits from her research program, a program he could not afford to carry out at his own greenhouse. I wanted to go to Mrs. Bowen and tell her what was going on, but I was afraid. If it came to a showdown, would she believe Mr. Gompers, or me? Though I felt I couldn't take a chance on telling her, at least I thought it only fair to correct those phony records. Now I defy you to tell me that putting *correct* information in a record book is a crime."

"No wonder," Nelson exclaimed, "Mr. Gompers was startled when he learned that his phony records had been removed and the correct information was inserted. He *had* to claim they were forgeries, because this information wouldn't connect up properly with things he had told Mrs. Bowen, and with markers and tags he put on different plants. A lot of them were wrong, but he was the only one who knew they were wrong."

"Except me," said Thorton.

"I don't believe he ever suspected you," Ted explained. "As you say, he thought you too stupid. The person he did suspect was Miss Lance. That is the reason, I suppose, that he called John Barley anonymously, and threatened his fiancée. He wanted to scare her off from reporting him to Mrs. Bowen."

"Wouldn't Miss Lance have reported to Mrs. Bowen right away?" asked Nelson. "Why would she bother to insert those forged sheets?"

"He must have felt that she had blackmail in mind. He expected her demands would come later, after she had him worked up into a proper frame of mind."

"Poor Clarice!" exclaimed Mrs. Bowen. "If he had known her better, he would have known that never in this world could she have done such a thing as that."

"You may be right, Mrs. Bowen," said Thorton. "I'm sorry I couldn't tell you about Mr. Gompers. It might mean the loss of my job, and that was an automatic one-way ticket back to prison. Who else besides Mrs. Bowen would take a chance on me?"

"What about that tank of poisonous spray?" asked Mr. Bowen.

"Well, I didn't think Mrs. Bowen would catch Mr. Gompers on those forged records, so I was wondering if I couldn't get him implicated in some other way. I was hoping to get him suspected of *something,* and then if Mrs. Bowen once had her thoughts turned in that direction, perhaps she might be able to put a few other small bits together and arrive at the truth. But I learned that she doesn't have that type of mind at all."

"You sure did make it look as though Mr. Gompers stole the poison," Nelson pointed out. "Who else could it be? The only trouble was that it was too obvious, and so nobody believed it."

"No, and that young man in the swamp didn't help things either. His meanderings helped divert attention away from the real culprit."

"Would it have been profitable for Mr. Gompers to steal things from you to help out his own operation?" Ted asked Mrs. Bowen.

"Oh, yes," she replied, "especially in its formative stages. I might try a thousand experiments, and only one is successful. But he might be in a position to tell me they had all failed, while he himself took the fruits. And of course he was in a position to get cuttings or maybe even whole plants that he needed to fulfill his own orders."

"What's going to happen to Mr. Gompers?" Nelson inquired.

"Why, I would simply discharge him and let that be the end of matters. Very many of these things would be difficult to prove. Ted has reasoned certain things out logically, but that isn't proof. Our biggest proof comes from Mr. Thorton, who would not, I am afraid, make a very creditable witness. But the Governor Hope rose is a very different matter. I have no doubt that Ted is correct, his patent application is already in. He will have priority, unless we can prove fraud, and that, I think, is what we shall have to do. I am sure my patent attorney will know the best way to proceed with the matter."

CHAPTER 18.

QUEEN OF THE SHOW

THE next day Nelson drew the car up to the curb, as close to the flower show as he could get, though it was a block away. He and Ted started to get out, but Buzz held back.

"Look, I'm not going into that show. You think I want to meet my mother in front of all those people? How do I know what's going to be said?"

Ted and Nelson looked at each other with some impatience. After all, Buzz had arranged this thing himself.

"I'm sure your mother won't say anything embarrassing in front of outsiders," Ted assured him.

"I know, I know, but the whole thing's kind of personal."

It looked to them as though Buzz was just making excuses. He seemed to be suffering from some sort of stage fright, and if they weren't careful he might decide to cut and run.

"What do you want us to do?" Nelson demanded.

"Look, can't you go in and ask her to come out? We can talk out here on the sidewalk without a lot of people around."

Nelson looked at Ted, who shrugged slightly to show they might as well do as Buzz suggested.

"All right, wait right here," Nelson ordered. "Don't move a step."

He and Ted then got out and walked rapidly toward the hall.

"I don't like this a bit," Nelson said. "If we don't get her out here double-quick, he's likely to head for the wide open spaces. I wonder what he's afraid of? Mrs. B. isn't an ogre."

"Don't you think he knows that? It isn't easy to face people who have been kind to you, after you've been ungrateful."

"I hope she's here and we can find her quick. If Buzz disappears again, we're going to be in real trouble with Mrs. B., and I wouldn't blame her a bit. We should have told her about Buzz as soon as we found out."

"Well, we can't undo that now."

They entered the hall which was well filled with visitors even though the hour was still early. The fragrance of scores and scores of roses on display filled the room, but they hardly noticed as they searched for Mrs. Bowen.

"I think I see her," said Ted suddenly. "Isn't that she up at the end of the aisle?"

"Looks like her, but who are all those people with her?"

They approached the little group ahead of them. Someone seemed to be carrying on an animated conversation with Mrs. Bowen.

Nelson put his restraining hand on Ted's arm. "I don't see how we can barge in there. Those people might be important."

"Remember how fidgety Buzz was when we left? Well, then."

Ted eased his way into the group. He hoped to catch Mrs. Bowen's eye, but that was impossible, for a man was speaking directly to her.

Then the man noticed him, and stopped speaking. Mrs. Bowen looked at him questioningly.

He tried to speak quietly but the entire group could hear him.

"Mrs. Bowen, there's someone waiting to see you outside."

She looked surprised. Couldn't it wait, or couldn't he have brought the person inside to her? Obviously, it couldn't wait, or Ted wouldn't have interrupted.

"Please excuse me," she said, and hurried away. Ted saw Nelson escort her toward the door.

When Nelson returned a few minutes later, Ted asked, "Did Mrs. B. make out all right with Buzz?"

"I didn't wait to see. From now on it's up to them."

They drifted along the aisles, admiring the gorgeous displays, but anxiously looking around for something else. Eventually they found the competition for the lavender hybrid teas.

"Ted! Isn't that the blue ribbon?"

"Sure is. But look at the notice. 'Governor Hope, exhibited by Mrs. Anya King.' They must have worked that out between them."

Nelson raised his eyes. "What's that plaque?"

"It's for Queen of the Show!"

They finally moved on reluctantly, for there were others waiting to approach the counter. Then they waited near the door. Soon they saw Buzz and Mrs. Bowen coming up the walk, arm in arm. Spotting them, mother and son came directly toward them.

"How's tricks?" asked Nelson.

"Can't you guess?" Buzz replied. "I'm back in the nursery business where I belong. I guess it was bred in me, though for a while I resented it."

"Then everything's all right?" Ted asked.

"You mean my legal troubles? We've decided to fight it. I know I was partly responsible for the accident, and I'm willing to make good on the damages to the car. But when they ask damages for injuries they never received, and threaten me with jail, I think it's time to fight."

"It was Buzz's own decision," said Mrs. Bowen with obvious pride, "but I think it was the right one."

"Somebody's waving at you," Nelson said. "Say, isn't that the governor?"

"It surely is, and he wants us to join him. Come along."

"Us too?" asked Nelson.

"Surely," and the group moved down the aisle to meet the governor.